WORLDWALKER

THE BANNERET SERIES

1

JAMIE DALTON

CONTENTS

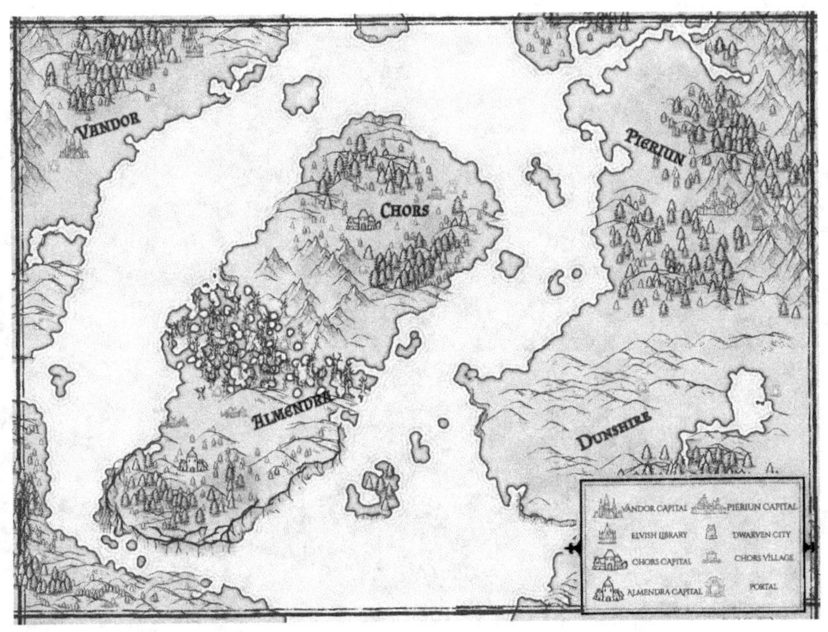

VANDOR
PIERIUN
CHORS
ALMENDRA
DUNSHIRE
VANDOR CAPITAL
PIERIUN CAPITAL
ELVISH LIBRARY
DWARVEN CITY
CHORS CAPITAL
CHORS VILLAGE
ALMENDRA CAPITAL
PORTAL

PROLOGUE

War rarely has a true victor. The ultimate widow-maker doesn't care which side a person is on, and those leading the charge often see their citizens as mere pawns. Such was the case for the kingdom of Pieriun. All hope had been lost when, centuries ago, a mad king and his daughter came up with an even madder plan—one that would stop the attacks, eliminate their threats at home, and leave their kingdom at ease. There remained no magic or practitioners of it, only humans carrying on a simple style of life.

The best laid plans don't always last forever, though. Time goes on and the natural order of things resets. For some, the war never ended; for others, it's only beginning.

"Did you hear that they found Jeb's body last night?"

The voice of Adalyn's best friend, Isabella, snapped her out of her daze. "Sorry, what?"

"Remember Jeb? He was new—mostly scrubbed pots and pans and unloaded deliveries." Isabella stood on the opposite side of the wooden table in the king's kitchen, her auburn curls dusted with flour. "They found him in an alley behind a pub. It seems he was on the bad end of a robbery gone wrong or something."

"Really? I thought he had just run off or decided he wasn't cut out for kitchen work. Poor Jeb." Adalyn eyed the empty spot near the door of the king's kitchen, wondering how Chef Staryn was taking the news. "Do you think it's why Chef took today off? He never takes a day off. When his sister got married, he had her schedule the wedding between meals so he didn't have to miss a day."

"I don't know. Are you all right?" Isabella asked. "You seem out of sorts."

Adalyn nodded and started kneading the dough in front of her again. Truth be told, she was exhausted. She'd been having the strangest dreams lately and woke up feeling almost as tired as she had been the night before. Nothing had worked to stop the dreams. Her lids grew heavy, and she caught herself dozing once.

When it happened again, her hands slipped off the pillowy dough and caught the lip of the bowl. A ripping sensation jerked through her body, and she watched the bowl flip and land on her own frame, which was now laid out below her on the stone floor. She held her hands out in front of her face, and her mind reeled as she stared at Isabella through them. Her spirit was no longer attached to her body! Looking around the king's kitchen, she watched her friends and other kitchen workers as they noticed her lying on the ground.

"Adalyn? *Adalyn!* Wake up!" Isabella cried out, scrambling around the table.

Something was pulling her spirit away from her body and leading her outside. With a last look at the crowd gathering around her motionless form, she followed it, preferring to go of her own free will rather than be dragged along. She didn't know what exactly was happening, but she hated feeling as if she wasn't in control.

Pushing herself through the city walls, she followed the pull past grassy meadows and into the forest surrounding the capital. Deeper and deeper she went, until the forest was so thick she could no longer see the bustling city behind her. Each tree she passed through sent a tingle through her. The pull became stronger the longer she took to get to her destination.

Finally, she stopped before a small clearing, the tug on her spirit easing. A group of individuals dressed in dark cloaks and masks gathered around a stone archway. They chanted in a language that sounded familiar, but she couldn't place it.

While floating above the group, she circled around, trying to see if she could identify any specific details about the individuals or what they were doing, but their cloaks and masks made that difficult. A glow appeared out of the corner of her eye. The keystone on the archway lit up, and each sequential stone radiated in a pale blue, becoming brighter as more stones ignited.

A teal mist in the form of a human head emerged from the stones, peering around. Stepping out, the figure stretched and seemed to take in a deep breath. Adalyn quickly spotted several more arms, legs, and heads of varying blue and green hues peeking out from inside the arch. Within seconds, a crowd of spirits meandered around the clearing, investigating the still-chanting group, who were clearly unaware of their visitors. Elves, humans, and several races that Adalyn didn't recognize gathered in groups of spirits. As they took in their surroundings, the same look of confusion befell all of their faces. Adalyn kept her distance from the spirits, the mystery of what she was experiencing making her wary.

Eventually, the chanters stopped, and one asked, "Did it work?"

"I don't know. I didn't notice anything different."

"Yeah, I didn't see any changes."

"Of course, it worked. You think I would have had us come all the way out here to cast if it wasn't going to?

Magic doesn't always have to be visible to work. The spells cast by the best sorcerers could rarely be seen by the human eye."

"No need to get testy, Nightshade. We aren't saying you don't know your stuff. It's just that, after so many years of working out the spell, that was a little anti-climactic."

Nightshade huffed.

A spirit stopped moving and looked up, the first to notice Adalyn floating above them. "Who are *you?*" Other spirits joined the first in staring quizzically up at her.

Feeling the pull return, she seized it and moved as quickly as she could away from the clearing, hoping this meant she really wasn't dead and could get back to her body. She had no idea if there were any consequences to being away from it for too long, and she had no desire to take that risk. The pull grew more urgent and swept her up, carrying her back to the kitchen and slamming her spirit back into her body.

Groaning, Adalyn turned her head and shifted to her side.

"Careful. Don't move too quickly." A doctor from the castle stopped her from sitting up and looked her over. "Are you hurt? How do you feel?"

Adalyn checked each part of her body with small movements, feeling for discomfort or any hindrance.

"I don't know." What had just happened? Was she ill? That would explain her strange dreaming, she supposed.

"Don't move yet. I have a stretcher coming. I want to take you to the infirmary to look you over more thoroughly before we release you. I'm insisting you take at least the rest of the day off. Where's Chef Staryn? I will tell that stubborn man myself."

Isabella's brows raised as she offered a reassuring touch of her hand. "It's his day off. He won't notice she's gone anyway."

The doctor nodded. "That's that, then. Has this ever happened before? Do you pass out often?"

"No, I don't..." Adalyn attempted as exhaustion and blackness crowded her mind and overtook her, "...think so."

ADALYN WOKE UP IN THE CASTLE INFIRMARY, confused, until she remembered the incident in the kitchen. Noting the dim light in the room, she realized the sun must have set some time ago. She shook her head and sat up as she thought about what had happened. It had to have been a dream. There's no way it could have been real.

She kicked her legs over the side of the bed and sat up. Her head in her hands, she contemplated lying back down and getting more sleep only to notice something was still in the bed next to her. Turning to get a better view in the dark, she realized that it was her—or at least, her body. There was no mistaking it. No one else in the castle had skin so pale it could almost glow in the dark.

Her mind raced as she tried to grasp what this meant. How could her spirit be outside of her body? Maybe it hadn't been a dream before. Adalyn glimpsed a faint glow out of the corner of her eye.

As the light floated toward her, she could almost make

out a shape. The image seemed familiar, but she couldn't place how.

A tall, beautiful man with long, silver hair and a dark aura approached her with the light and offered his hand. "Let me help you, young one. I am Venlian. It is time for you to remember."

She grabbed his hand and allowed him to pull her away. Then fear struck her heart as they moved too far too fast, and she tried to return to her body.

"Don't worry, you will come back. It is not yet your time."

That didn't comfort her in any way, but after a few moments of struggling, she watched as the world took form in the night around them. He led her to a building made of a shimmering gray material with large cathedral windows and a deep black roof. They passed room after room quickly, so she only managed glimpses of the mysteries inside each one before being led away and past the next.

Rooms filled with mirrors showed reflections of objects which weren't there. A music room had melodies playing but no one to play them. Room after room of peculiarities passed until they finally entered what looked like a library.

The most extravagant and peculiar library she had ever seen, with unbelievably tall walls lined with floor-to-ceiling bookshelves, drew her in. Glowing spheres hung from the ceiling, casting a kaleidoscope of different shapes and colors, and an odd variety of the most elegant yet comfortable-looking chairs and tables she had ever seen sat in front of the windows.

Her mysterious guide spoke. "Herein lies the history of your people, and of my people. In your dreams, you have come here and seen this. You have seen me. You have explored these shelves, but you don't remember fully, do you?"

Images flashed through Adalyn's mind, and she blinked in an effort to clear them. "I thought they were dreams."

"No, not dreams. Something even better." Venlian gestured to the shelves around them, and an image—a memory?—of him doing so another time crossed Adalyn's mind. "In these books are the histories of individuals, the stories of their lives."

"Is there one for me? Could I see it?"

"All of your kind are among these books, but I am afraid peeking at your own would be unwise. It is not yet complete. It is dangerous to open the book of someone whose story is unfinished, and should only be done in extraordinary circumstances."

"Unfinished? What do you mean?"

"It would be easier to show you than attempt to explain."

He pulled down an old, tattered book and opened it. Inside were words and images as she expected, but they didn't stay put on the page. Adalyn reached forward to touch the book and was startled to find that her hand moved through the page and occupied a space inside that the thickness of the book couldn't possibly contain. Moving her hand, images and words swirled around, reminding her of a bowl of soup.

"I don't understand."

"This library is the result of a spell cast by a very powerful elf long ago. When a person is born, it creates a book which holds all of the possibilities that person's life can hold. If a book is searched while a person is still alive, parts of their story could be altered or even go missing. These books are connected to the individual's fate. The one you are holding is of someone in the past. You can't change a dead person's past, but can change a living one's future."

Quickly pulling her hand out, she looked up at him. "Why did you bring me here?"

An almost sad, distant look haunted his eyes. "With the old ways appearing in your world again, it is time to return something that has been hidden here for centuries. Things have been broken, but not yet shattered, and everything is about to change." He reached inside the book and pulled out a short sword inscribed with ancient lettering. Setting it down on the table, he reached back in and pulled out a key.

"This sword belonged to one of the Banneret. Keep it by your side and learn to use it. It will be one of the only defenses against the things awakening in your world. It has magical abilities that the human world has long thought destroyed and forgotten." He held out the other object. "This key belonged to the old king. It opens a part of the castle that has been locked away for many years. Give it to your king. It is now time to reopen old secrets. It is the only way for things to be right again."

Adalyn fumbled with the artifacts, surprised when Venlian put them in her hands. She wasn't sure how she'd been able to pass right through walls but could now hold these items.

"Why are you giving these to me? Wouldn't it be easier if you found and gave them to the Banneret or the king yourself?"

"The Banneret disappeared from your land long ago, and it is not time yet for me to see the king. This sword is not like others. Only you can use it to its fullest, just as only the king can use the key. The sword can only be used by those who have the same abilities as the one who forged it."

"I don't have any abilities, though."

A smile cleared some of the darkness from his face. "Do you see any other humans here? You have a special aptitude for crossing worlds, an ability known by the Banneret as worldwalking. Which worlds you can cross into will depend on what your needs are at the time and where you want to go. In your dreams, you are not limited, and have been to many worlds and realms. That is why you feel as if you remember this place and remember me, but don't know how. After you have been somewhere while awake, you can return at any time without guidance."

"You're right, I feel as if I've been here before. Wait, is that what happened yesterday? When I was pulled from my body to a stone archway?"

His brow raised as he quickly opened and closed his mouth. Shaking his head, he replied, "It's why you haven't been able to sleep as well. As your ability developed, you started to wander. It's easiest for your spirit to slip from your body while you sleep. Tell me about this stone archway you saw."

Adalyn did so, questioning only briefly her sudden trust in this man. Memories she had pushed away as strange dreams were returning to the front of her mind, and she told herself she'd process each of them when she had some quiet moments.

Venlian listened to her tale intently, only interrupting her occasionally to ask clarifying questions.

"You have given me much to think about," he said when she'd finished. "Keep this sword near you, and it will help control your ability as you learn how to use it yourself. Long ago, there were better resources for your training, but much has been hidden from humans in your world for far too long."

"Humans? You make it sound as though you're not human."

He tucked his hair behind his pointed ear. "That's because I'm not."

She should have guessed that he wasn't human. She had never met anyone quite like him in the capital. "Weren't all non-human people wiped out over five hundred years ago?"

"Not all of us, as your people were led to believe." Venlian turned toward the door, and his eyes became distant again. "It appears that our time has been cut short. Remember what you've been told and what you need to do. If not, all will be lost."

Adalyn felt a tug from afar and, with a nod, let her spirit be pulled back even faster than when she'd left. She groaned as her spirit slammed back into her body again.

Voices whispered with each other near the hearth as someone stoked the fire and hung a kettle over it. It was still dark out, and all she wanted was sleep. Something poked her as she rolled over away from the fire. She reached to move whatever it was and pulled up a sword with a key on a leather cord wrapped around the sheath. Her heart stuttered in her chest. It wasn't just a dream. She stared at the items in the weak firelight, somehow finding comfort in them. Her lids grew heavy, and she let them close, hoping she could finally get some sleep.

TWO

"Good morning, everyone," Chef Staryn boomed, which was followed by a chorus of much less enthusiastic greetings from his bleary-eyed helpers. "We are expecting the queen's mother and sisters to arrive for a visit in four days. That means extra places to set as well as extra requests."

Adalyn and Isabella exchanged a knowing glance.

The last time the queen's family came to the castle was for the wedding. One of the sisters didn't eat meat while another insisted she was allergic to sugar. Everyone knew she had a stash of chocolate in her trunk, but that fact was unspoken. This visit would last even longer than the previous. The queen's baby wasn't due for another month, and her family planned to stay until after the birth.

Chef's voice pulled her back into the moment. "We have a lot of preparations to make before they arrive. The queen has also requested a private meal for herself and the king tonight." He looked over his staff, noting their varying degrees of attentiveness to his speech. "I need a volunteer to gather extra supplies, things we don't have in the gardens here."

Adalyn shot her hand up. "I'll do it!"

With a raised brow, Chef gave her a once over. "Why are you wearing a sword? Actually, it doesn't matter. I don't have time for frivolities. Just don't let it get in the way." Chef handed the list over, looking away as if already thinking about the next task. "Take this and head out right away. Find me when you return for your next assignment."

Isabella nudged Adalyn. "If only I was so fortunate to have claimed the task first."

"I'll be thinking about you when I'm out in the fresh air, enjoying the sunshine," she replied with a wink.

Adalyn found most of the things on Chef's list fairly easily at the market, but the last item was outside the city. It seemed the queen was craving a particular kind of sweets, and the person who made them lived in the nearby woods and only occasionally came to the market, preferring the quiet there over the hustle and bustle of the capital.

Out of the city, the warm breeze held the sweet smell of coming rain. After fetching the sweets, Adalyn basked in the sunshine as she walked back, enjoying the rare opportunity for a walk in nature. A creek burbled near the path, and she stopped for a drink.

Crouching, she set her basket down and scooped a sip of water in her hands. Without warning, she felt a push from behind—a force knocking her into the water and holding her under. Arms flailing and legs kicking, she tried to push herself off the bottom of the creek, but whatever held her down was too strong. Her vision grew dark, and for a moment, the thought crossed her mind that this was the end of her.

In a last attempt, she let her body go limp with the hope that whoever was holding her under would believe her dead. The hands that held her underwater were suddenly removed, and she surfaced, gasping. She pulled herself out of the creek and looked behind her to find a man fighting a tall, ghastly figure. Gray skin hung from a thin torso, and a gaunt, haggard face revealed sharp teeth and pointy ears. Its eyes were clouded as a foul smell wafted over, making her gag. None of the man's hits seemed to affect the creature.

The two bashed against each other, and the creature knocked the man down. He slid across the grass on his back. His sword flew from his hand and into the woods out of reach.

Glad that she had chosen to follow Venlian's advice, but sure she must be absolutely mad because she had no clue how to use it, Adalyn unsheathed her sword and charged at the creature. It swatted at her without looking in her direction and sent her and her sword flying back and apart.

The man on the ground rolled and picked up her sword. In one swoop, he spun back and stabbed upwards into the creature's chest. It cried out and slumped to the ground beside him.

The man sat up, wiped her blade on the grass, and returned it to Adalyn. "How did that happen?"

"I don't know, but it doesn't look like it was from around here."

He shot her a look, clearly wondering if she was a fool. "That was a death slaugh, a dark fairy who has been cursed. I meant, how was your sword able to kill it when my own had no effect?"

"I truly have no clue." Nodding in his direction she asked, "How do you know what it was?"

He walked over to pick up his sword and glanced around the clearing, "They're featured in children's tales where I come from. It's hard to forget the face of something that haunted your dreams for years."

"But it's huge! It was taller than you—I thought fairies were tiny little things."

"Different types of fairies are different sizes. Unfortunately, the darker they are, the bigger they are. This one's been following me for a time. I've been evading it, hoping to avoid a fight, but then it attacked you." The man looked Adalyn up and down. "Where are you heading?"

"I work at the castle. I came out here on an errand."

The man sheathed his sword and glanced at her items strewn around the creek's edge. "I would feel more comfortable if you would allow me to escort you back. I don't know if it's more for your safety or my own conscience, but either way, I would prefer it if I could. I'm heading that way anyway."

Giving him a look, she decided he didn't look too untrustworthy (he had saved her life, after all) and nodded his direction. "Let me gather my things, and then we can go. I'm Adalyn, by the way."

He glanced back at her while pacing around the creek, looking for any other threats. "Nolan. We should hurry. I am scouting ahead of someone and need to get to the castle myself."

As she wrung out her cloak, she paused with a realization. "You're traveling with the queen's mother?"

Nolan stopped and looked at her, slightly surprised. "I am. She is a day behind me."

"I work in the king's kitchen, and we've been preparing for her arrival. I thought she wasn't coming for a few more days, though."

"I think she was getting antsy. This is her first grandchild, after all."

"Of course." Having gathered everything, Adalyn started walking back along the trail, and Nolan fell in beside her. "I'm surprised you were sent ahead alone. I would think that you would have had at least a few people with you."

"I prefer to travel alone. It's easier to go unnoticed, and I have the skills to protect myself if needed."

Adalyn had watched the castle guards practicing in the courtyard, and having seen Nolan's swordsmanship, she didn't doubt that he was as good as he claimed.

"Where have you been? And why do you look like you went for a swim?" Isabella asked, arms folded, looking at Adalyn's damp clothes and wild hair. She'd seen Adalyn leave her basket in the kitchen when she returned to the castle and followed her to their shared room.

Digging through her drawers to find dry clothes, Adalyn responded, "Well, I can promise that it wasn't an intentional swim. Hand me a dry towel, and I will share some exciting news with you before I tell Chef."

Isabella tossed a towel over. "I'm all ears."

Not quite sure how to start, Adalyn began with what was easiest. "The queen's mother will be arriving tomorrow."

"Early? Chef is going to freak out."

"I know. I'm heading down there next to give him the news. I'm sure that Nolan will have told the king by now, and Chef may have already been informed, but just in case…"

Isabella grabbed Adalyn's hand. "Wait, who's Nolan?"

"Only a knight in shining armor who rode in on a white horse and saved me."

Isabella stared dumbfounded. "You're kidding, right?"

"Only a little. There was no white horse or anything. He's a scout for the queen's mother." Adalyn told Isabella the whole story, beginning with her errand outside the city. Isabella was an attentive listener, gasping and looking shocked at the appropriate places, but her first question startled Adalyn.

"Is he cute?"

"Really? I tell you I was attacked by a death slaugh, and all you want to know is if my rescuer is cute?" Adalyn huffed. "I don't know. Maybe? I really didn't think about it too much. I was a little too busy trying to stay alive."

"Priorities. Besides, you look well enough now. And this man saved you from that wild animal or whatever. I need more details about him. What does he look like?" Isabella's eyes were wide, and her cheeks ruddy.

Shaking her head, Adalyn pulled on a fresh tunic.

"Well, he's tall, with light brown hair, and tanned skin, which I guess isn't really a surprise since he has been traveling. He looks strong. I really wasn't looking at him the way you would. Anyway, I'm ready. Want to come with me to talk to Chef?"

"Sure! This should be entertaining. I wouldn't want to miss this conversation."

The kitchen was fairly empty as the two arrived. A worker prepared food under Chef Staryn's watchful eye, but they had another hour before the majority of the cooking began for supper.

Placing the basket on the table in front of Chef, Adalyn cleared her throat to get his attention. "I think I got everything you asked for."

He shuffled through the basket. "What about the Corsa mushrooms? Did you not find any?"

"The vendor didn't have any, so I got a different kind as replacement."

Chef grumbled as he looked through the other contents of the basket. "At least you got the sweets for the queen. I still haven't found out why she is so particular about getting them from this one person."

"I also found out that the queen's mother will be arriving tomorrow, ahead of schedule."

"What? How in the world did you discover that?"

"When I was down by the creek, I was attacked."

He straightened and ran his eyes up and down her body. "Are you all right? You don't look harmed."

"I'm fine."

He lifted a brow and his lips thinned. His expression told her he didn't quite believe her.

"I swear, I'm not injured in any way. One of the queen's guards showed up and helped me out."

His eyes widened for half a moment before they narrowed on her. "What was the queen's guard doing out in the forest? She shouldn't be wandering in her condition."

Adalyn noted Isabella's big grin and the fact that she was basically bouncing on her toes, and mentally kicked herself for her backwards storytelling. "Not our queen, Chef. Her mother's guard. He was scouting ahead, and rescued me when I was attacked."

Chef seemed to process this information for a moment, then grabbed a piece of paper and a quill and started writing.

Isabella leaned over to see what he was scribbling. "What's that?"

"A list of tasks that need to be completed today. If the queen's mother is showing up tomorrow, we have a lot to do. When everyone gets back in here, I want to have assignments ready." He paused and looked Adalyn in the eye. "I really am glad you're safe. You've worked for me for, what, four years now?"

"Almost five, ever since I came here from school. I'm glad you took a chance on someone so young."

"I could see that life had forced you to grow up quickly. Even at fourteen, you were one of my most reliable workers. It is to your advantage that you learn quickly. Look at you now. You could practically run this kitchen yourself if you had to."

Isabella laughed. "Don't go telling her that. She has enough pride as it is."

Shaking his head, Chef jotted down another task. "I don't know. Adalyn's got the skills. I just may have a way to take a vacation someday. I've always wanted to see the coast."

Adalyn fanned herself as she blushed from the attention. "You two are clearly out of your heads. Chef, no one could or should ever replace you. I don't mind helping here and there so you can have some time off, but this kitchen is all yours. There are plenty of people working here who are much more skilled than I. John's fantastic at pastries, and Ruby works wonders with roasted meats. Isabella, the way you transform vegetables into something that even I want to eat is basically magic."

Chef's face lit up with a warm smile that reached his chocolate brown eyes. "The fact that you can recognize those qualities in others is exactly why you could run this kitchen someday."

Looking away from the two of them, Adalyn brushed imaginary crumbs off the table. "It's fortunate that won't be an option for quite some time, right, Chef?"

He shrugged, and turned his attention back to his paper. "Obviously."

Sensing Adalyn's discomfort, Isabella pointed to the list. "Right, what can we do to help? We're here a bit early, so we could get started on what needs to be done."

Only paying half of her attention to the rest of their conversation, Adalyn took a deep breath to settle herself. She appreciated the vote of confidence that Chef Staryn had in her, but she was relieved that there were plenty of others with much more experience and skills who could take over when the time came.

THREE

The rest of the day was a whirlwind of trying to get everything ready for the queen's mother to arrive with her party. Now it was just a waiting game. The queen's mother, a queen herself, was due to arrive any moment. Adalyn took in a deep breath of fresh air, standing on the balcony of the castle. She wanted a good view when the caravan arrived.

The capital had an artistic charm that other cities simply did not. Most cities were boxy and sterile-feeling due to old buildings being torn down and rebuilt, but not the capital.

The castle had the best view. It was built into the mountain with its turrets being all that told the eye where the mountain ended and the building began. Waterfalls on the east side of the castle flowed into canals that ran through the city alongside old cobblestone streets with ancient but well-kept buildings, each with its own variety of stained-glass windows and different shades of blue roofs. It almost seemed as if the capital was a river itself, flowing from the castle. It was truly beautiful.

Closing her eyes to take a deep breath and enjoy the calm before the storm, Adalyn opened them to a commotion near the city gates. It looked like the caravan was finally here. She had heard stories about Queen May's family, and it was hard not to believe them.

The queen herself was always full of energy and didn't seem constrained by societal expectations. It was said that's why King Coeus had married her. Her home kingdom was nomadic and oftentimes called eccentric, but the arrival of one of their caravans was always anticipated, as they brought a feeling of festivity wherever they went.

Looking at the procession coming up to the capital, those stories seemed to fit. Not only were they wearing bold, bright colors and textures that most people would avoid, but their carts and horses were adorned the same.

Something was wrong, though. There were bodies in the carts, and their attitude was somber, a drastic change from their usual frivolity. A large crowd gathered around the party as enforcers escorted them the rest of the way up to the castle. With a worried gasp, Adalyn turned to head inside. She would be needed in the kitchen with the party here, and it looked like they might need medicinal herbs, or at least some comfort foods.

"WHAT DID YOU DO?" ISABELLA ASKED A WHILE LATER, shooting a knowing look at Adalyn.

Trying to blink the tears from her eyes, Adalyn set

down her knife from chopping onions. "What do you mean, what did I do?"

"The king asked for you. The king, himself. He never talks to people who aren't known to be important."

"I honestly have no idea. Want to go in my stead?" Adalyn responded jokingly as she dried her eyes with a corner of her apron.

"Oh, of course, that would go well. He would never know."

Pushing the door open while untying her apron, Adalyn just laughed. "If I'm not back by midnight, send out a search party."

"A search party? I will be raiding the chocolate you've got stashed in your drawers if you aren't back by midnight. Someone else can bother with a search party."

Stepping into the hall to start her way to the king's meeting room, her hands trembled a bit. Joking aside, she was nervous. Everything she had done recently ran through her head. Why would the king want to talk to her? She kept out of trouble and did her job well. It was unusual for the king to even worry over the problems of people in as low a position as hers. That was Chef's job. An image of the pale-haired man popped in her head as she handled the key in her pocket. She should have found a moment to request an audience with the king before this, but had been too scared.

With each step, she told herself everything was all right. Taking deep breaths, she tried to slow her racing heart. This couldn't be about the key, could it? There had to be something else. Stopping at the door, she reached to knock just as it swung open. Adalyn jumped back.

"Nolan?"

His hand still on the handle of the door, he gave her a slight smile. "Adalyn, just who I was going to look for. Come in."

"Why were you looking for me?"

"I will let the king explain."

She followed him into the room and jumped at the sound of the heavy doors closing behind her. Bowing low, Adalyn prayed she wouldn't fall over while waiting to be recognized.

The king waited a moment, looking her over. "Adalyn Mernt?"

Straightening, Adalyn responded, "Yes, Your Majesty. That's me." She glanced at the other people in the room, recognizing some of the advisors.

It seemed she would get no further introduction.

"I'm assuming you've heard what happened to the queen's mother's party on the way here?" King Coeus asked.

"Um, I'm afraid not. I did see that they were in distress as they came into the city."

"They were attacked."

Adalyn gasped, her eyes wide. "That's awful!"

"Nolan tells me you were attacked just outside of the city yesterday, as well."

"That's correct, I was."

"These two instances happening so near to each other, and during a time of peace, seems too coincidental to me. What can you tell me about it?"

She related her tale to the king, then glanced over at

Nolan. "I think you called the creature that attacked me a death slaugh?"

Nolan nodded. "It was."

The king leaned toward Nolan. "How do you know it was a death slaugh? They're a myth—really, a fairy tale that we tell children to make them behave. The stories were once possibly based on truth, but probably greatly exaggerated."

Nolan locked eyes with the king. "I promise you, that creature was no myth. It was definitely a death slaugh. My family has very old drawings from when they walked our world, and it could not be mistaken."

"That's... disheartening." King Coeus shifted on his throne. "How did you overpower it, then? If I remember correctly, the stories say they can't be killed with an ordinary weapon once they've been revived from their slumbering state."

Adalyn fiddled with her hands a bit. "It didn't seem to take damage from Nolan's regular weapon. He was able to stop it with my sword."

"Where is this sword?" the king asked.

Of course, this would be the one time that she decided not to wear it. It just felt silly to when she had no clue how to use it. "In my room. If you would like, I can go get it for you."

"No, you stay here. I have more questions for you. I will send someone to fetch it while we talk." He motioned to someone, and they stepped out to see it done.

Looking up, Adalyn remembered the key for the king. "Your Majesty, I was actually given something to pass along to you." Pulling the key from her pocket, she stepped forward. "I was told to give you this—that you would need it."

Brow furrowed, the king motioned for a guard to take the key. "How did you get this?"

Her voice became as small as she wished she could be in that moment, "If I told you, I doubt you would believe me."

Another guard returned with Adalyn's sword and placed it on the table in front of the king. He narrowed his eyes at her. "I'm assuming you don't wish to tell me where you got this, either."

She shifted where she stood and shrugged. "The same place I got the key?"

He gave her a momentary glance with his brow raised. Tenderly touching the sword's hilt, King Coeus suddenly pulled back his hand, then gazed more intently at the weapon. "Do you know what this sword is?"

"I was told it was a Banneret sword."

The king mumbled to himself. "I want to think it's a fake, but it just stung me." He motioned for the guard to hand him the key. "It was said that the Banneret had special swords that claimed their owners, and that they were forged with magic. I always thought the stories were just tales, but between your sword burning me and the death slaugh's sudden appearance, I have no choice but to speculate about the possibilities. I need to know how these things came to be in your possession."

Adalyn swallowed nervously, but seeing no alternative, she launched into her story. Murmurs rustled the air around her as she told about her spiritual wanderings and meeting with Venlian, but the king stayed silent, watching her with a look she couldn't read.

"What does it mean, all of this showing up now?" she asked when she'd finished.

King Coeus shook his head. "I'm not sure, but I think we're in trouble if we don't figure it out soon."

FOUR

After a thorough interrogation, Adalyn was dismissed from her meeting with the king and sent back to the kitchen. She relished in the busy atmosphere over the next few days, finding comfort in the familiar work while her mind turned over the strange things she'd experienced lately. With the queen's family settled in, Adalyn couldn't help but shake her head at the girls in the kitchen swooning each time Nolan came in with special requests. No matter how many times Chef told him there was no need to make the trip, he persisted. Adalyn wondered if these special trips were for his personal enjoyment or as a request from one person in particular.

Focusing on the exact angle she was cutting the carrots, she chose not to look up after seeing him enter the kitchen for the third time that day. After talking with Chef, he moseyed over to her, flashing his charming grin to the blushing girls as he passed by.

"Want any help? I'm quite skilled with a blade."

She glanced up at him while continuing her work. "I remember. You seem quite handy with a sword, but I'm afraid the exactness of these cuts with a little bitty knife may be too much for you to handle. I guess that's to be expected from someone who is part of a queen's traveling guard. Only good for the big, messy jobs." She couldn't help but smile a bit as his eyes lit up at her teasing. "How long have you been in her service?"

"It feels like I've been involved in one way or another my whole life. My family has always served. Both of my parents were protectors of the family. It's all I ever wanted to do. Have you always wanted to be a cook?"

Her board full, she scraped the pile into a bowl and paused before grabbing the next bunch. "I've always enjoyed cooking, but really found my way to the capital out of necessity."

"Really? How's that?"

"My parents disappeared when I was younger. We lived in the mountains away from most people. My parents are merchants and liked having a peaceful retreat from their travels. It was a quiet life. When I was old enough, I was sent to a nearby town for school. I returned on vacation when I was thirteen to find my parents had disappeared. I haven't seen them since. With them gone and having no other family, the money they had set aside only covered another two years of school, so I set out to find work afterward. I had learned a few skills, and figured that the capital would be my best bet for finding something that could keep me housed and fed. I never dreamed I would get to work in the castle."

He moved his hand towards her but pulled it back

before making contact, "I'm sorry to hear about your family. How long have you been working here?

Noting the movement, she gave him a smile, "I've been here almost five years. It's good work. Chef is fair, and there's always something new to learn or do with the visiting dignitaries coming through."

"I guess that explains why you were so terrible with your sword," Nolan chuckled. "I was afraid you were going to hit me with that thing!"

Adalyn laughed as well, "Let's just say it was my first time wielding a blade that big. I use knives in the kitchen all of the time, but a sword is heavier and feels just a bit different."

Nolan nodded. "Perhaps there is something we can do about that."

"Get up, Miss Mernt. The hit wasn't too hard. Pay closer attention to your footwork and run through that again."

Adalyn shot a dirty look across the yard at the sword master while slowly pushing herself back up for the millionth time that day.

Not long after the king discovered that she had the first Banneret's sword, Adalyn had been required to train daily. Whether Nolan had a hand in it, she didn't know, but the visiting queen had decided to take advantage of the long stay and had several of her men training as well. For the past three weeks, it had been early morning training followed by a long day in the kitchen. Isabella teased her mercilessly about it as she woke her each morning, and Adalyn cursed her lot at sharing rooms with an early bird. How could her friend be so chipper in the morning? She awoke each day so sore, just rolling out of bed hurt.

A hand reached down to help her up, turning Adalyn's thoughts back to the present. "Don't feel too bad. You're actually doing well, considering the brief time you've been handling a sword. I promise you've improved a great deal since the first time I saw you with it." Nolan wore his usual smirk, but she couldn't help but be grateful for his help pulling her back up.

"I'm not so sure about that. I feel like I have noodle arms and can barely hold my sword up by the end of practice."

"What happened to those amazing skills with a blade you were bragging about?"

She shot him a dirty look. "Look, I can't imagine actually dueling someone. Maybe I should give up on this and train with daggers instead. I imagine those would feel more familiar in my hands."

"That's part of the problem. What will you do the next time you run into a death slaugh? How about if you run into one of the people who is reviving them? Have you thought about that?"

Kicking the ground, Adalyn looked down, slightly embarrassed. "Well, no. I guess I just never thought I would have to worry about it. I work in the kitchen."

"Yes, but I'm sure you didn't get that sword just so you could chop carrots with it."

Adalyn knew he was right, even if she didn't like it.

After a deep breath, she readied her sword, and Nolan came at her with his. She continued to work through the motions of blocking Nolan's advances, but she was knocked back onto the ground again.

Sitting there to catch her breath for a moment, she asked, "So, your queen's family is nomadic, right?"

"We are. We travel pretty much year-round across the kingdom."

She cocked her head, "But they are royalty and have a set area of land. Don't they have an estate that they can live in?"

Nolan threw his head back, his body shaking from laughter. "We don't travel because we have to, but because it is a way of life that has served us well. During the Great War, the Dunshire people served as spies. Due to our nomadic nature, we were able to move around without being out of place, and are trained in combat from a very young age."

"I never knew that. It's been five hundred years since the Great War, though. Has no one since then decided to settle down over all those years?"

"Many of our people stay put for at least part of the year, raising crops and such, but wandering is in our blood, and even farmers spend part of the year traveling. The ruling family still prefers to travel most of the time. Queen Tillie believes that seeing to things herself is better for the land. No one questions it, because the profits of our kingdom are much higher than most, without much in the way of rebellion over the past five centuries. Queen May learned many things from journeying with her mother that prepared her for ruling with King Coeus."

"That's interesting. Give me your hand. I'm ready for another…"

Adalyn paused, her hand in his, and turned toward shouts from beyond the wall. The commotion grew louder, and everyone in the yard stopped what they were doing. Guards at the gates shouted that the castle was under attack.

The sword master sprang into action. "My men, to me!" The men in the training yard grabbed their weapons and surged towards the gate.

Nolan grabbed Adalyn's arm and lifted her up before dragging her toward the castle. Confusion gripped her. "What are you doing? Where are we going?"

"We need to get to Queen May. She is due any day, and won't be able to move quickly, let alone defend herself properly. Queen Tillie is with her, and it's my duty to protect her."

Adalyn knew he was right and followed closely. Glancing back, she saw the sword master engaging with men in heavy armor. The country hadn't experienced conflict for quite some time, so the first two gates were customarily left open during the day. Clearly, that had been an error, as the invaders had broken through the third gate and flooded in. Their crest, an eye over a V inside a circle, triggered a memory, but now wasn't the time to determine why. She pushed forward and entered the halls as guards hurried to close the doors and bar them.

Running up the stairs that led toward the queen's corridors, servants were pushing inward while soldiers rushed down to head off the invaders. Looking down the halls between staircases, she noticed some individuals were standing still in the middle of the halls, looking panicked, until others pulled them along.

They dashed up three flights of stairs, Nolan pushing through anyone who interrupted his path, with Adalyn close behind.

Coming out of the stairs to a landing, they came upon a group of soldiers guarding the floor. Nolan tried to push through them. "Let us through. I need to get to the queen."

A soldier barked back, "We were instructed not to let anyone through. You can help guard here or go help at the gates."

"You will *not* stop my own guard from reaching me." A demanding woman spoke from behind the guards. This must be Queen Tillie. "Nolan, come through *now*."

The men parted, and as Nolan stepped through, Adalyn followed.

Hurrying down the hall toward the queen's chamber, the queen's mother spoke to Nolan. "What is the situation? What's going on out there?"

"The castle is under attack," he replied. "I don't know who it is, but they are well trained and in great numbers. They were breaking into the courtyard when we were entering the castle. I think we need to move Queen May as quickly as we can. In her state, it will take her a while to get anywhere safe."

"Where would we take her, though?" Queen Tillie asked.

"I work in the kitchens," Adalyn piped up. "I know of

some tunnels that lead under the castle and into the mountain. There are food stores in the tunnels, and very few know of their existence. They would be safer than the castle."

Entering her daughter's chambers, the queen's mother stopped and looked Adalyn over, making a decision. "If you can lead the way, let's do it." As she turned to give orders to those in the room to prepare to leave, the king entered with his guards. He must have been in a meeting with his advisors, for many of them were with him.

"They've made it onto the first floor. Our men can't hold those numbers back for long."

"A plan to retreat is already in motion," Queen Tillie responded. "We are leaving now."

"Where to?"

"This young woman says there are tunnels under the castle and into the mountain. We just have to reach the kitchen to get to them."

All eyes turned to Adalyn, and she rushed to explain, "I know there are exits from those, and we should be safe for the time being as long as we seal up the entrances behind us."

The king nodded. "I concur. The tunnels have been used for this purpose in the past and should serve us well. Are you ready, my dear?"

Queen May waddled over toward her husband, escorted by several handmaidens. "As ready as I ever will be."

Adalyn led the party back into the hall and toward the servants' stairs leading down toward the kitchen. The queen was trying to keep up, completely out of breath, and the king and his men surrounded the group.

On the last flight of stairs before the kitchen, everyone froze momentarily when a loud clang followed by a yell came from below. Adalyn, Nolan, and several guards rushed down and walked in on a towering creature knocking a man across the room.

The smell of blood hit Adalyn's stomach, causing it to turn. "It's a death slaugh! How did one get in here?"

Nolan pushed her back towards the stairs and rushed in to attack, closely followed by several of the king's men. The death slaugh let out a roar as it lashed out with its long, gray arms and sharp, yellowed claws. The skin hung from its bones, and blood dripped from its fangs.

The group attacked, but their hits didn't seem to affect the creature. Remembering then that her sword was the only thing to harm the last one, Adalyn pulled it out of its scabbard. Inching forward, she looked for an opening. Nolan saw what she was about and fought harder to keep the beast distracted.

Raising her sword, Adalyn readied herself to deal a blow with all of her strength, but the death slaugh turned and knocked her down on her back.

Ignoring the others, it quickly moved in for a killing blow. Adalyn's sword suddenly felt lighter in her grasp. Her mind calmed, and as if someone else was moving her body, she gripped the sword and forced it toward the death slaugh. After the sword dug deep into its belly, the monster slumped and sagged onto her body with dead weight.

The strange calm left her, and she panicked. "I'm stuck! Someone! I can't breathe!"

Nolan and several soldiers rushed to pull it off of her and helped her to her feet. "Are you all right?"

"For now, at least. My head is killing me, and I'm not sure about a few ribs, but we can take care of those when we get to safety." She grabbed a nearby rag and cleaned the foul-smelling ichor of the monster from her hands and sword. After she replaced it in her sheath, she winced as she rubbed her ribs.

Nolan nodded, and Adalyn headed toward the back of the kitchen as the rest of their entourage poured in. Opening the door to the cold storage room, she walked in and beckoned for the rest to follow.

"Close the door, please. This next part won't open as long as that door is ajar."

Someone closed the door, plummeting the room into darkness. Reaching next to a shelf, Adalyn released a lever. The shelves inched forward, and Adalyn pulled with every bit of strength she had left to move them and open the hidden door behind it.

Stepping beyond the door, her eyes adjusted enough to make out the torches and light one, illuminating a narrow stone corridor. The rest of the party followed into the hall, and a guard closed the hidden door behind them, securing the bar across it to prevent anyone from following them.

Slowly working their way down the hall, they finally came upon another door. Opening it revealed a room with bags of grain and beans and bottled goods on shelves. Adalyn turned toward the guards.

"There is another room on the left where some furniture is stored, and then more tunnels. We should be safe here. The queen needs to rest." Suddenly, the world shifted, her vision darkened, and she stumbled toward the wall, sliding down as everything went black.

"We need to find a way out of these tunnels!" a man's voice bellowed.

"Yes, sir, I know," came the placating reply. "It's just that so many of the tunnels have collapsed. It's going to take a while."

"I understand that, but if we don't find a way out, we will all die." The first man's voice had taken on a bit of a whimper compared to his bellow before.

"Will you stop it? Enough with the gloom," a third man scolded. "Try doing something useful for once!"

Adalyn groaned as she started coming to. The sound of everyone's voices made her head hurt. Rolling over, she suppressed a cry from pain, having forgotten about her bruises. Slowly, it all came back to her.

"Easy now. Don't try moving around too much yet," Nolan said, handing her some water. "How are you feeling?"

Adalyn groaned again and took the canteen. "Like I'm back from the dead. How long was I out?"

"Only a short time. You seem to have some pretty big bumps and bruises, but nothing too bad. I think you'll make it." His concerned face softened with a slight twinkle in his eye.

Oh, how that grin killed her sometimes. It was more of a smirk, really, with a dimple showing on his left side when he was amused. The smile lines around his eyes made her melt a little inside even when he wasn't smiling. Shifting to sit up, she looked over at the king and his men to see them huddled over old maps.

"How much ground have you covered so far? I take it you haven't found a way out yet."

"Not yet. We were hoping you could help us out with that."

"I'm afraid I'm not going to be much help there. I know there are tunnels that lead out because that's how we had our stockrooms filled, but I was never involved with that process. I can help look around, though."

Nolan put his hand on her shoulder, stopping her from rising. "Finish your water first. A couple more minutes won't hurt anyone. Take your time getting up, and come find me when you are ready."

Adalyn watched Nolan get up and join the king's conversation. His confident gait left her wondering how he could always be so positive. As she drank her water, she looked around. Someone must have found the stored furniture and brought some chairs in, as the queens and their attendants were sitting in a group. There were fewer men present, so some must have gone to explore the tunnels.

Finished with her drink, Adalyn slowly got to her feet

and moved her limbs experimentally. The movement didn't cause her more pain, and she was relieved. She walked around the room, noting the ingredients on the shelves. When there was nothing else to look at, she waited in the corner for Nolan to have a break in his conversation.

Eventually, she grew bored. She stole another glance at Nolan. It didn't seem like he would be finished anytime soon. Tired of waiting, but not wanting to disturb Nolan, she decided to explore the tunnels nearby on her own.

Gathering her belongings and a lantern, she crept out the door and into the hall, letting her feet carry her into the tunnels with no set course in mind. She could see what the man had meant about some of the tunnels being blocked. Not all of them were, but enough had caved in that she had to retrace her steps often after coming to dead-ends. Once in a while, she came across a few men from their group as they searched.

As she ventured deeper into the tunnels, stopping to glance into the rooms, she noticed that the architecture of the halls was changing. Closer to the castle and the room everyone sheltered in, the halls had finished edges and ornate scrolling carved on pillars and doorways. Those disappeared as she went on, and new shapes were beginning to show up. They were more geometric and rigid, but beautiful all the same. Even the color of the stone was changing, turning blue-gray the deeper she got.

After what felt like forever, she came to a crossroads, giving her three choices of where to go. None seemed more promising than the other, and by this point, she had become so turned around that she couldn't remember exactly how she had gotten there or which way to go to head back.

Movement to her left caught her attention. Turning, she lifted her lantern to light as far down that path as possible. Nothing. Sighing, she turned around and decided to go down another path.

Suddenly, a face appeared only inches from her nose. Her heart jumped in her chest, and she squeaked out a small scream. The person who had startled her looked strange, and upon closer inspection, Adalyn realized she could see through… the ghost? The edges were blurred, and it looked almost as if it were laughing at her.

"Who are you, and what do you want?" Adalyn asked, trying to make herself look and sound as intimidating as possible.

The individual's lips moved to speak, but Adalyn couldn't hear anything.

She tried to focus on the being in front of her, and her head began to hurt again. "What?"

A whisper of a voice slowly grew louder as she focused on it.

"I said, you seem lost."

"Well, I guess." Maybe she had lost her mind along with her sense of direction.

The ghost smiled down at her. "So, you can hear me now. You've been ignoring me for a while."

Slowly, the image in front of her became more clear, revealing an older woman dressed in a black and blue uniform, her white hair in a long braid down her back.

"I'm sorry. I honestly didn't know anyone was there. Who are you? *What* are you?"

"I'm like you. Well, at least I was. I was the last Banneret with your ability."

"But you're dead… right?"

"Of sorts. It's complicated, but to make things simpler, you can just say I'm dead."

"And why are you following me?"

"To help you. You're really very close."

"Close to what? Please say an exit."

"Of sorts. If you would have seen me sooner, I could have made this process much simpler."

"I still don't understand what is going on. Why couldn't I see you sooner?"

"You weren't using your ability. You are a worldwalker, yes? I'm just in a world that is parallel to this one. When you were straining to see further down the hall, you unknowingly saw partway into the world I'm in as well."

"You're in a parallel world? I thought you said you were dead."

"It's… complicated. Over time, you will understand a bit better, but for now, let's get you where you need to be before you overextend yourself. I remember just how tiring using my ability was when I was first learning."

With a glance that said there was no wiggle room for disobedience, she turned around and headed down a path, waving for Adalyn to follow. Still slightly in shock that she was following orders from a ghost, she paused before following the woman.

"So, you were a Banneret with my ability?"

"I was. I guess I still am, in a way."

"What's your name?"

"Glenda."

"It's nice to meet you, Glenda. I'm Adalyn."

Glenda chuckled. "I know."

They continued walking down the hall in silence for a long while, leaving Adalyn wondering how much Glenda knew about her and how. Still not entirely convinced that Glenda was someone she could trust, she opted not to ask. She had a feeling that the more she asked Glenda, the more questions she would have. Plus, she didn't like the idea of someone knowing things about her already without her knowledge.

Suddenly, Glenda stopped in the middle of the hall and turned to face the wall on the left. "Open it."

Adalyn looked at the wall, puzzled, seeing nothing to open. "Open what?"

"Use your ability and look at the wall. You will see what you need to do."

She turned to look at the wall again, and her headache became worse as she focused intently on the space in front of her. She could see something now. It was faint, but there was an outline of a door, and one stone looked darker than the rest. She reached up to touch it, and the door groaned open, allowing the scent of dank air to escape.

"Who would make a door that no one can see? That's kind of silly. It defeats the purpose, doesn't it?"

Glenda looked over at her, shaking her head. "When will you learn? Why share something out in the open that you want hidden? Besides, it wasn't always that your world didn't have magic in it. There was a time when many could see this door. Enter, and you will see what I mean."

Adalyn gripped the edges of the stone door, and it slid

open easily. Much to her surprise, lights illuminated a massive room behind it. Bookcases lined the walls, and a large fireplace and oversized furniture filled one side of the room, while the other was piled with trunks and boxes.

"What is this place?"

"This was the Banneret's room. It's where we spent our time when we were off duty. Before the Great War, many of the staff lived in these tunnels, including the Banneret. When we saw that our way of life was disappearing, we hid it all in here."

"It's... incredible. But why did you bring me here?"

"To show you something else. Something that your world has forgotten."

"This seems to be a common occurrence for me recently," Adalyn mumbled, remembering Venlian and the elvish library.

Glenda walked to the piles of trunks, weaving among them to reach the back wall. Reaching out to a tapestry hanging there, she looked back at Adalyn. "Behind here. This is what you need to see."

Following Glenda's path to the wall, Adalyn pulled the tapestry to the side, revealing a large metal door with a keyhole but no handle.

"It's locked. I can't get in."

With folded arms and a look that told Adalyn she was missing something obvious, Glenda nodded at the door. "I've been watching you and have seen that you've done some worldwalking in your spiritual form. Now you need to learn to do it with your physical body. Focus your energies on where you need your body to be."

Adalyn wasn't sure what exactly to do. Did she just

wish herself there? Maybe imagine herself going through the door? She decided to try that and concentrated as hard as she could while touching the door, to no avail. Her body hadn't moved an inch.

An idea struck her—maybe the other side of the door looked just like this side. Focusing on an image of what she hoped was the other side of the door, she felt herself almost becoming lighter. Seeing a light in front of her, she kept the image of the door in her head and willed herself toward the light, her head feeling like it might burst. Suddenly, she felt a snap around her and saw that she was no longer in the room but instead in another hallway leading away from the door.

"Well done! How did your first time physically world-walking feel?"

She leaned on the wall, holding her stomach as her vision blurred. "It could have been better."

Glenda looked at her with concern. "I can see that I've pushed you a bit too far. I will stay with you as you continue on, so you can let me out of your vision for now. Just remember that you aren't alone."

As Glenda's image began to dissipate, the headache eased, leaving Adalyn only as exhausted as she was when she had led the king out of the castle. Turning down the stairwell, she made her way down a seemingly endless flight of steps. The ceiling gradually rose higher and higher until no longer in view. The sound of water nearby grew louder as she continued down the path until it opened up into an incredibly vast cavern.

Faintly glowing rocks illuminated a city before her. Unbelievably tall pillars lined a road to the center of the city and back out into a pinwheel of roads from that point. A tall statue of a well-built man with an unruly beard holding an axe in one hand and a hammer in the other stood in the middle of the road with a pool around it.

The flat area around the city center was dotted with small homes and open markets. Buildings grew larger as they climbed the cliffs of the cavern. Everything was still, quiet, and empty. Wandering around the city, Adalyn couldn't help but wonder what had happened to the people who lived here. Who could have lived in such a place and thrived, and why had they abandoned it?

She chose to climb up the sides of the cliffs to explore some of the buildings toward the top, when a small cry followed by the sound of pebbles falling caught her attention. Slowly, she crouched down and walked closer to where the sounds came from, trying not to make any noise herself.

She drew in a breath and rushed over when she saw two very small children, one trying to pull up the other from a ledge. It seemed the city wasn't completely abandoned after all.

"Let me help."

She reached down and lifted the one hanging, setting him on the ledge beside the other. "Are you all right? Where are your parents?"

Both stared at her with wide eyes and then took off running. Getting up, she followed them through several buildings and watched them slip through a crack in the rock wall. Trying to make herself as small as possible, she got on her hands and knees and followed them, only to be hit over the head as she reached the other side.

"Ow! That hurt! Why would you…" Her voice left her when she looked up to find a group of short and stocky men looming over her. The children hid behind them.

"Be quiet," the shortest of the men replied to her gruffly. Looking over at the children, he nodded. "This is why it's dangerous to go into the ruins. They are forbidden for a reason." He addressed one of the men next. "Take them back to their parents and let them know where these two were."

Obviously, this small man was in charge of the group. The remaining men crossed their arms, stepping closer to her.

Adalyn, still crouched on the ground, spoke up. "I wasn't trying to hurt them. One had fallen, and I helped him up. I wanted to make sure that they were all right."

The group of men eyed her with suspicion, and the leader spoke again. "How did you find us? Where do you come from?"

"I followed the tunnels."

"All tunnels leading here from above ground are sealed. How did you find us?"

"I swear! I followed the tunnels and found a door that led to you. I'm from the capital of Pieriun. I work in the king's kitchen."

One of the other men grumbled, "She's a spy. They must be digging through our blockades to try to find us."

The leader glared at her as he thought for a moment. "It's been many years since we were last hunted. Still, I don't trust her. Take her to the cells. We can question her there."

Large, calloused hands took hold of her shirt and pulled her the rest of the way out of the crack while another pair of hands took her sword from where it was strapped to her side.

A loud clang caused Adalyn to stop resisting for a moment.

"You clumsy fool. Pick that up," the short man barked at a shocked-looking, auburn-haired man.

The auburn-haired man's face morphed into a challenge, "You pick it up. That thing just stung me."

"That's not possible. I said pick it up."

Shaking his head, the auburn man backed away, his eyes glancing between the sword and the extra short man. "Nope. Not worth it, sir."

A growl rumbled from the shortest man as he reached down to pick up the sword by its hilt, only to quickly shift into a yelp as it fell back to the ground. Adalyn tried to stifle a chuckle. The sword seemed to have a mind of its own regarding who handled it.

One of the men handed their leader his cloak to pick up and wrap the sword in. A smug smile and nod of his head told her that he clearly thought he had just won a great victory and signaled for her captors to start moving.

Pushing her in front of them, they forced her through a gathering crowd of short, stocky people and toward what she assumed must be a jail of some sort.

"Why is everyone here so short?"

A shove from behind pushed her hard enough she almost fell. "I thought you were told to be quiet. Dwarves are not forgiving people and don't like to have to say things twice."

She couldn't believe it. Dwarves! They were only a myth, but so were death slaughs and elves, and she had seen both within the past few weeks.

The cell turned out to be among three others, with a small table and chairs for the guards across from them. There were no other occupants, and it seemed the cells weren't used often. Adalyn kept watch of the one carrying her sword as she was tossed on the hard ground, only to despair as she saw it being carried out of the room. Even if she could escape, there was no way for her to get her sword as well.

Her headache began to worsen again, and a faint voice was talking to her from inside the cell. Remembering that Glenda had said she wouldn't leave her side, Adalyn looked closer until she found her leaning against the bars.

"Don't despair. You found what I sent you to find. Go back to your king and bring him. He has the key to the door and will need the dwarves' help to regain his kingdom."

"How do you know?" Adalyn whispered, trying to not draw attention to herself.

"I see much more than you could possibly know in this world."

As Adalyn was about to say she couldn't get out, she remembered how she'd gotten past the locked door to get here. An idea formed, and Glenda grinned, seeing that she had figured it out and remembered on her own.

Trying to picture a room that she had only been in once before wasn't the easiest thing to do, but she closed her eyes and tried to remember every detail she could. She could feel herself becoming lighter, but didn't see the light. Second-guessing herself and her memory, she suddenly thought of Nolan and pictured him in the room, his dimples when he smiled, and the way he teased her. A friendly face that brought peace in her heart and butterflies in her stomach.

The light appeared in her mind and steadily grew brighter as she remembered their conversation. Trying to remember the smells and sounds of people moving around, she was pulled forward and snapped back into feeling whole again. Opening her eyes, she was happy to realize she had done it! She had worldwalked from the cell back to the storage room near the castle.

Suddenly, it dawned on her that maybe showing up in the room itself wasn't such a great plan. No one knew of her new ability, as she had only figured it out a short time earlier. The looks on everyone's face in the dead silence confirmed that this probably wasn't the best idea. If the wide eyes and dropped jaws told her anything, it was that there was no hiding her newest ability from the king and his men now.

"Well, aren't you an unexpected thing? It seems that Pieriun is no longer without magic," Queen Tillie said with an inexplicable twinkle in her eye.

Adalyn fidgeted with her fingers as she waited to see what would happen, taking note that the king and those from Dunshire recovered much more quickly to her sudden appearance in the middle of the room than those from her own kingdom.

"W-w-what just happened? Where did she come from?" a skinny man with day-old copper scruff asked.

"You're a worldwalker," Queen May said in a quiet voice.

Looking surprised, King Coeus quickly turned towards his wife. "You know about this?" He clearly hadn't briefed her on the subject.

"It's not like you know everything about my home-land. I'm surprised that you knew about this," she said with a mischievous grin.

Nolan hurried to Adalyn, a look of concern on his face as she wavered where she stood. "Are you all right? You look pale."

Adalyn was sure she did. She had been exhausted while following Glenda, but this last jump from her cell to this room took what little she had left.

"I just… need to sit down for a minute."

Nolan guided her to a nearby chair where she sat, head in her hands.

King Coeus approached her. "What happened?"

"I was looking around nearby and got lost."

Adalyn refused to make eye contact with Nolan. She already knew what his expression would be after not waiting for him.

"You got lost, so you used your ability to get back here?" King Coeus asked.

"Not exactly. I went further than I meant to and ran into someone who showed me a room… actually, that reminds me!" Adalyn looked up at the king. "Do you have that key I gave you?"

"I do."

"Great, I know where it goes."

"Where is that?"

"It unlocks a door to the dwarves."

A few snickers and murmurs echoed from the others listening in on the conversation. It all stopped when the king pointedly cleared his throat.

"You saw dwarves?"

She nodded her head enthusiastically and instantly regretted it. "That's where I was before I came here. I was in one of their cells."

King Coeus pulled a chair over and sat down near Adalyn. "Start from the beginning. What exactly happened?"

Adalyn told him everything—about meeting Glenda, finding the Banneret's room, the underground city, and being captured by the dwarves. Once she was done, she waited to see the king's reaction.

"Do you think that the dwarves are hostile?" he asked.

Adalyn thought for a moment, then shook her head. "I know they were scared. Throwing me in a cell wasn't because they wanted to attack me. I think it was fear of the unknown. If they've been down there since the Great War, the last time they saw any humans, they were being hunted by them."

King Coeus leaned back in his chair while stroking his short beard. "I think we need to meet them. If they've been living here—literally under our noses—all this time, they've had ample opportunity to come against us, but haven't. We need to find out if they are a potential ally, especially now, when we've been attacked and need all the friends we can find. At the least, they may be able to help us find our way out of these tunnels."

"We can send a party down. Some soldiers and a few of us," one of the king's advisors offered.

The king nodded. "Let's do that. I need a few volunteers to come with me; the rest will stay with Queen May. Lieutenant Vaeren, organize the volunteers and prepare to leave in an hour."

"Me, sir?" the skinny man asked with a slight quiver.

King Coeus shot him a look.

"Of course, we will be ready," the man quickly corrected himself.

"Your Majesty, I think it would be best if you stayed behind. It's not safe to have you heading into potential enemy territory like this," another of the advisors interjected.

King Coeus held up the key that Adalyn had given him. "If there wasn't a reason for me to go down there, it wouldn't have been important to get me this key. It could have gone to anyone."

"What if something happens to you? Lieutenant Vaeren can go in your stead as a member of your court, or perhaps one of us?"

"If you make sure that my wife and child are safe, there will be an heir. It's my responsibility to make sure that there's a kingdom to be heir to. I'm going, and that's final."

"If I may," Queen Tillie spoke up, "I would like Nolan to accompany you; as a representative from my own king-dom, but also as an extra layer of protection. He's quite proficient."

The king looked at Nolan. "Agreed, he can come as well."

As everyone began to prepare, Adalyn eyed a pile of grain sacks in the corner and quietly worked her way over to lay down on it. She knew she would need Glenda's help to find her way back, and there was no way she could handle the extra strain of using her ability again without at least a short nap.

"It's not too much farther. Just around the corner and down a bit." Adalyn was glad Glenda had stayed with her and led her back. She'd forgotten just how lost she had been before. There was no way she could have found the Banneret's room again on her own.

The woman's appearance after they left the queens had been such a relief. She never spoke to Adalyn, but would appear when needed to show a turn, and occasionally Adalyn saw her walking among the group. These small glimpses helped Adalyn feel confident as she led the way, and she was relieved to find they didn't tax her strength much.

Stopping in the hall, Adalyn told them, "We're here."

The group of men looked around, then back at her like she was crazy. "Where, exactly, are we?" the king asked.

Instead of answering, she reached up and pressed the stone to open the hidden door and stepped inside. The group followed her and began to spread out, looking at things more closely.

The king stopped just inside the door. "So, this is where the Banneret lived." He wore a pondering expression as he took in the perfectly preserved artifacts around him.

Walking over to the tapestry, Adalyn pulled it aside to unveil the locked door. "Do you have the key I gave you?"

He traced her steps through the piles and pulled out the key, putting it into the lock and turning. They stepped back as the door groaned open, revealing the tunnel beyond.

Adalyn stepped into the passageway and started down the path while the rest of the men followed behind. Leading them deeper into the mountain and down into the abandoned city, she stopped at the entrance and watched the faces of the men, knowing hers had to have had the same expression not too long ago. After a moment, she led them toward the crack where she'd come upon the dwarves.

Nearing the place, a dwarf appeared, then another and another, until they were surrounded by a large group of short, stocky men wielding heavy weapons. Recognizing one of them as the leader of the group from earlier, Adalyn pointed him out to the king with a murmured explanation.

"You must be some special kind of stupid, human," growled the dwarf. "Earlier today, you were our prisoner. Somehow, you escaped, and then came back thinking to attack us? We've stayed hidden from you humans for over five hundred years, and now that you've found us, you think you can come here and wipe out the rest of us. I can promise you that we will not be taken down so easily!"

"We are not here to harm you," the king said, his tone carefully moderated. "I am Coeus, King of Pieriun. We came into the tunnels to escape from an attack and seek the dwarves' aid."

"Hah! And why should I believe that? My people have lived in fear for five centuries because of your kind."

The dwarves were pressing closer, and the king's men bristled as they prepared to defend themselves.

"Now, Fostrin Goldbow, is this how you greet visitors? Let alone a king?"

Adalyn knew that voice, but it seemed out of place. There was no way it could be—but there he was. Venlian stood beyond the group of dwarves to their rear, his gaze fixed on their leader. How the person who had told her she was a worldwalker could be here was beyond comprehension, but a very welcome surprise.

Fostrin snorted. "What do you think you're doing here, elf? This is not your kingdom. You have no say here."

"True, but how do you think King Thanmog will react when he discovers that you attacked the king of the human realm above when he came in peace?" Venlian asked as he wove through the circle of dwarves to stand near King Coeus.

It was obvious that Fostrin didn't like Venlian but knew better than to challenge him. "As you wish. Human king, we will escort you to our king. Don't even think about trying anything." He turned and begrudgingly motioned the group forward.

Glancing at Venlian as she walked, Adalyn found him watching her. She mouthed the words *thank you* to him and fell in line behind her group as she prepared for the worst but hoped for the best. She had escaped from the dwarves' cells not too long ago, after all, and wasn't sure how the dwarf king felt about that.

King Thanmog's palace was not what Adalyn would have expected from a royal. It seemed that all of the dwarves lived along what looked like a ravine, with homes carved into the cliffs on either side and bridges crossing back and forth from one side to the other. The palace was no different from any other home on the outside. A taller doorway than most, but otherwise very unassuming.

Geometric carvings embellished the rock wall around the doorway, but once they stepped inside, the space opened up completely. High arches with stocky, carved pillars opened up to a large great room. As the guards guided them toward what Adalyn suspected was the throne room, it was difficult not to stop and gawk at the battle scenes carved into the walls and ceilings. Compared to her kingdom's castle, there was practically no gold leafing or tapestries. Instead, everything was highly polished stone, so glossy that if the light shone on it just right, it could almost blind you.

Their group stopped in front of a door, and Fostrin gave three heavy knocks. A guard on the other side immediately opened it a few inches, and the two men whispered back and forth. The door shut again, and the group waited. A moment later, the door opened wide, and the guards gestured for them to enter.

They approached the dwarf king on his throne, stopping some paces from it, and the dwarves and elf bowed while the humans stood tall.

"Who do we have here?" King Thanmog asked, a brow arched as he leaned to one side.

Fostrin answered, "This is Coeus of Pieriun, sire, the human king from the city above, and his people. I believe you are familiar with Venlian, Keeper of the Tomes."

King Thanmog looked the group over for a moment, then nodded once to King Coeus before addressing Venlian.

"It's good to see you again, old friend."

"And I, you," Venlian replied with a slight bow. "I would like to introduce you to King Coeus of the Pieriun kingdom. He and his people have not come with any ill will."

"King of Pieriun… the last time our people met, yours slaughtered most of mine. We went into hiding, but you have found us after all this time. How?"

"Our castle was attacked, and we were forced to retreat into these tunnels," King Coeus responded. "One of my people was exploring and came upon your abandoned city earlier today. Your existence here was discovered while searching for a way out."

King Thanmog scratched his beard and shifted a bit in his throne. "I had heard that a human escaped from our cells, simply vanishing even as the guards looked on. Our world was sealed away with magic, and I was led to believe all humans with those capabilities disappeared long ago. So, tell me, how is this possible?"

Every human present, including the king, looked at Adalyn. "I believe I can help with that," she squeaked out. "I was led here by, um, a ghost. A Banneret from the past named Glenda. I have some… abilities which made it possible."

"I assume that those abilities are also how you escaped from our cells, as well?"

"Yes."

"It seems that magic is returning to the humans. I must admit that puts my mind somewhat at ease. Venlian, you say that these humans are to be trusted?"

"I do. I have been watching their kingdom from afar for some time, and I believe that you can help each other.

I was acquainted with the Banneret Glenda in the days of the Great War, and know of Adalyn's abilities."

"You've never led me wrong, Venlian, so I will take your word. King Coeus of Pieriun, if you will give me your solemn oath that you and your people will bring no harm upon my kingdom, we will shelter and aid you for a time as we are able."

Putting a fist to his heart, King Coeus bowed to the dwarven ruler. "I swear it."

That seemed to satisfy King Thanmog. "I have some matters to attend to, but I will have you and your men fed and taken care of until I am free to discuss how we may help each other."

King Coeus nodded. "I thank you. May I impose further on your hospitality by bringing the rest of my party here? We came to you with a small group only, leaving behind my wife, who is heavy with child, and her mother, Queen Tillie of Dunshire."

The dwarven king nodded his agreement and looked to his commander. "Fostrin, make our guests comfortable," and, nodding toward Adalyn, added, "and return this one's sword to her as soon as possible. We don't keep trophies of encounters from our allies, no matter how unique they may be." He said the last while holding King Coeus' gaze.

Fostrin only nodded his compliance and turned to do as his king had commanded.

SEVEN

Adalyn couldn't help but wonder how the dwarves were able to have fresh meat and vegetables. They had been living underground for so long, how could they have any outside connections? The food was delicious, and the dwarves were much friendlier than expected.

One dwarf in particular, Eridu Earthhand, the city's historian, was especially welcoming. She had been asked to tend to the humans while the kings discussed business, but she genuinely seemed interested in their lives and in them as individuals. Over lunch, Eridu helped fill in some gaps, explaining why the humans believed that dwarves were extinct.

More than five hundred years ago, during the Great War, the Pieriun king tried to extinguish all magical life, but the dwarves fought back. He feared his enemy would be able to use all magical beings the way they had used the fairies, which were captured, enslaved, and turned into death slaughs. Even though dwarves did not hold the same affinity for magic as fairies and humans, they were capable of manipulating magical objects, and therefore considered a threat.

Due to continued losses in battles, the dwarves' numbers dwindled. Dwarves do not reproduce at the same rate as humans do, and after losing too many battles to the human king, they devised a plan to go into hiding.

The injured and dying were sent into the main city, with the remainder of their people hiding in old caves they had enchanted to remain hidden. When the king attacked, he believed he had wiped out all of the dwarves that were left.

"We hold a vigil every year to honor their sacrifice," Eridu said. "We regret the necessity of it but are grateful for the safety we've had because of it. We don't live in the old city, fearing what would happen if humans found us thriving there."

Adalyn mulled over this new information. "I understand why your people locked me up when they saw me. I would feel the same way. I know your people sealed themselves away, but do you know anything about how the war ended? Our people are taught of the Great War and how all magic was wiped out, but no one ever speaks of how the war was won."

"I'm afraid I am not sure how the war amongst humans ended. When we sealed ourselves off, it was complete for us. Perhaps our elven friend could fill us in with some of the details. Venlian?"

Venlian appeared introspective. "Even my people do not know how your war ended. We had withdrawn to our home by then. I remember when the war began, the dwarves and elves were divided. Some clans supported Dragmire, the Pieriun king, who had an alliance with Dunshire, while others supported the other human kingdom."

"Wait a minute. You mean to tell me that the Great War was fought between humans, and then the battles humans fought against dwarves and elves happened at the end of it?" Nolan asked. "We were always taught that the Great War was between humans and elves and dwarves. Who were these other humans that we were fighting, and why were we fighting them?"

"King Dragmire was fighting another kingdom called Chors. There was drama around a broken marriage contract, and they attacked Pieriun. Dragmire was losing the war, however. The people of Chors had incredible magical abilities. Perhaps this is why he turned against all magic and believed it to be a threat."

Adalyn, who had been watching Venlian closely, came to a realization. "Venlian, you speak of this as if you were there."

Turning to face her, he responded, "That's because I was. The elven people live much longer than any other. We've witnessed the rise and fall of many kingdoms."

Trying not to let her jaw drop, she blurted out what seemed to be the only logical follow-up. "Whose side were you on?"

"It was difficult for any magical being to make the choice to join either side. In the end, I joined the ranks of the Pieriun army. Because of my knowledge, I was part of the council. I watched as King Dragmire unraveled and eventually decided to eliminate what he considered to be his biggest threat."

"You mean magic?"

"The people of Chors are from a different world and require gateways, which funnel their magical essence, to transport them from their kingdom to yours. He needed to cut them off, so he sought to close the gateways and eliminate all magic that could resist him."

Thinking about the Great War turned Adalyn's mind to their present struggle. Their kingdom had been attacked; was it possible an old enemy had returned?

"Did Chors have an emblem?" she asked. "The people who attacked the castle wore one. An eye was nested into the top of a V, with a circle around all of it. Does that mean they're from Chors?"

Venlian considered her with all the expression of a stoic, then gave the simplest of answers. "Yes."

Adalyn looked over the table to find its occupants wide eyed and slack jawed. What Venlian had disclosed was hard to believe. It was completely different from everything she had been taught.

Eridu shook her head and spoke. "I've read that King Dragmire was a crazed man, but that puts things in a new perspective."

"He wasn't always so unpleasant. His daughter was scorned, and his response, initially, was in support of her. The two of them became obsessed with the need for revenge and ultimately chose a rather unfortunate ending for the magic users of your kingdom."

"How did you escape?"

"I could see how irrational the king's decisions were

becoming. With each battle fought, he became more unhinged. Eventually, he and his daughter refused to listen to advice, and I took my leave."

"They just let you leave? In the middle of the war?"

"You say that like I gave them a choice."

For a moment, she had forgotten that he was an elf. Of course, he could come and go as he pleased. She had no idea what magical abilities the elves actually had, but if his sudden appearance earlier in the day had proven anything, it was that he had no issue traveling long distances very quickly.

"Did you ever check in after you left to see what had happened?"

He shook his head. "All elves and magical beings stayed in their territories and closed their borders. We had no desire to be part of the witch hunt happening here. For a long time, I didn't even read the more recent additions to my library."

"When did the elves decide to become involved again?" Adalyn asked.

"Today is the first time an elf has stepped foot out of our land in five hundred years. We have everything we need, and the world had become a very dark place. We live a very long time, and my life had become routine until a short time ago."

"If no elves have left in that long, how do the dwarves know you?"

"Just because we didn't leave doesn't mean we don't have ways to communicate with others. When something of note would appear in the books in my library, I occasionally would make a call to advise."

"A call?"

"We have these basins filled with a golden liquid…" Eridu started.

Adalyn jumped, startled by Eridu's voice. She had all but forgotten that the rest of the group was there.

"It changes color when someone tries to contact us, and we can communicate through them," Eridu finished.

Venlian nodded. "We placed them in all of the kingdoms to help us communicate more quickly."

"What did you discover that made you come now, then?"

With a serious gaze, he locked eyes with her and simply stated, "You."

EIGHT

The royalty spent most of the day behind closed doors with their advisors, and Venlian joined in their meetings after lunch. The dwarves hosted a reception for their guests that evening, and the kings stood to address everyone present.

"A day that began in fear at the meeting of our peoples is now one that we will celebrate!" King Thanmog boomed. "King Coeus and I have joined our kingdoms with an alliance, and the dwarves are free to live openly again."

"We've come to an accord," King Coeus added. "The dwarves will help Pieriun reclaim our kingdom if we first help them obtain something that can help us all."

King Thanmog's grin almost doubled at that statement. "As we are now, we would have little hope of being successful. However, if what King Coeus says is true, then I believe that we may be able to awaken our golems."

A little gasp escaped from Eridu. "But how? They are in Chors!"

"Not all of them. Quite a number are still here, but their keystones are missing. If death slaughs have been spotted in our world, the gateways must somehow be open again. We will send a group to recover the keystones we need, and the golems will be awakened."

"Death slaughs?" Eridu murmured, her face pale.

"Venlian has used his resources to verify that the spell preventing travel to Chors has been weakened, and we should be able to pass through our gateway in the old city." Both kings took their seats after this.

Nolan looked completely baffled as he tried to take everything in. "I think I'm missing something. Chors is another world. I get that it's been blocked by a spell all this time, but how would we get there? Is that even possible?"

Hands folded behind his back, Venlian turned only his head to look at Nolan. "Technically, it's just a kingdom on a different island. The distance is great, though, and the spell I spoke of has made it impossible to access since the war ended, moving the island to another world. With its weakening, however, traveling there seems plausible. The dwarves' gateway just needs to be opened."

"Any idea as to how we will do that?"

Venlian turned toward Adalyn. "I know exactly how we will do that."

Adalyn froze, her insides tense as she realized what he was suggesting.

IT QUICKLY BECAME APPARENT THAT THE MEETINGS that had kept the kings and advisors busy all day had been extremely productive in regard to the journey. It had been decided that only a small party would venture into Chors in an effort to go quickly and undetected. As she'd suspected, Adalyn would be using her worldwalking abilities to take them through the gateway. Eridu, as historian, had the best understanding of where and how to obtain the keystones for the golems and would be their guide, with Venlian's assistance, as he'd been to Chors before. Nolan would provide protection with Lieutenant Vaeren. Adalyn remembered the skinny man from their time in the tunnels and wondered how much protection he could really provide. She'd heard that Vaeren was a longtime friend of the king, so she shrugged and decided she'd just have to trust King Coeus' judgment.

With only a small group traveling light, their physical needs were minimal and easily prepared, and by the next afternoon, they were ready to depart. Mentally, Adalyn's mind was a whirl as she struggled to keep up with all that had happened thus far. She felt wholly unprepared for her role on the expedition. She'd only just learned how to take her body along when worldwalking. How could she now take four other people to a distant place she hadn't even heard of until the previous day?

There was no time to consider the answer, as she and the others were soon led down a narrow stone path. Their footsteps echoed, but no one spoke, making Adalyn's insides twist even more. She wasn't sure if she was more afraid of being successful or of failing.

The path ended at a small cavern with piles of recently excavated rocks surrounding the entrance, making Adalyn wonder if they were trying to keep someone out or keep someone in. The only detail in the cavern was a wall covered with both dwarven and elvish markings, creating an arch. Letters inside the archway changed shape in front of their eyes, shifting so quickly they were impossible to read.

"Are you ready?" Venlian asked, reaching out a hand to Adalyn and directing her toward the arch.

"I guess. I'm really not sure what I'm supposed to do."

"I know you've never been properly trained in how to use your ability, but you have used it enough that you should have some control over it. Touch the center of the arch, and you will be shown what to do to share your energy. I will keep my connection to you to help direct the door to open where we want since you have never been there before."

Tentatively reaching out toward the letters, Adalyn felt her fingertips warm as her brain became fuzzy. The shapes on the wall stopped shifting as she came into contact with them, and they formed words she could read. Preparing to speak the words that appeared with her contact, a surge of energy burst from her, pushing everyone back and causing Venlian to break his connection.

Whispers from the gateway spoke the words written there.

United among heart, sight, and life. Open to repair the broken beyond.

Golden light flowed from the outside markings on the wall, moving toward the archway until they poured down like a waterfall without a pool. Where there had been only a stone wall before, there was now a passage of light filling the arch.

Without thinking, Adalyn gave in to the magnetic pull and stepped into the light. For a moment, she was blinded by the golden energy flowing around her, and she stumbled forward until she felt grass beneath her feet.

Looking up, she was confused for a moment.

A grunt came from behind as another body stumbled into her. Nolan had come through the gate. Adalyn grabbed his arm and moved both of them out of the way so as to not be in the way of the others coming through. A moment later, Eridu and Venlian joined them, with Vaeren stepping through just before the gateway closed.

Venlian verified that everyone had made it there in one piece, and then glanced at Adalyn. "Well done, young one. You have a much larger reservoir of magic than I thought." He looked directly into her eyes for a moment, then turned toward Eridu. "Eridu, our guide, point us in the right direction. We should get started on our journey before it gets dark so that we can be away from the gate when setting up camp."

The look he'd given Adalyn was filled with unspoken words. Venlian was hiding something, but Adalyn could tell she wouldn't get any answers from him at that moment. She decided to let it drop—for now.

NINE

Adalyn was grateful to have the job of camp cook for this part of the expedition. She had no idea how to set up a tent or rig a perimeter warning system. While preparing the evening meal, she was in her element, and the familiarity of the task was comforting.

By the time her fire was going and a simple but hearty stew was on, the rest of camp was put together and everyone had gathered close. Giving dinner a stir, Adalyn's thoughts went to her friends in the castle. It had been just over a day, but she had no way of knowing if anyone had survived the attack. Was Isabella still alive, and if so, was she free, or was she held captive? If she was, this mission of theirs was the only way of freeing her friend.

Heaving a heartfelt sigh, Adalyn turned to Eridu. "So, we're here to do something about your golems. What exactly are we looking for?"

Eridu leaned back on a log and pulled a book out of her bag, opening it and showing a sketch to the group. "We're looking for the keystones. Our golems are unable to wake without one. During the Great War, the keystones were stolen and brought back to Chors."

"*Back* to Chors? They had been here before?"

"This is where dwarves are originally from. Most still live in Chors. Only a few groups such as ours had ventured to Pieriun to mine stones that don't exist here."

"If this is where dwarves originated, how did the golems end up in Pieriun?"

"Golems are… complex." Turning to another page with several sketches of large stone figures, Eridu pointed at one. "See, they are so much more than just large fighting machines. If a dwarf accomplishes something in their life that is extraordinary or highly beneficial to the dwarven race, they are offered the opportunity to become a golem. This way, they can continue to benefit society as a whole. They choose how they will look and what abilities they will have, and when they feel it is time, they undergo the transformation. Very few know how it's done, but what I do know is that once their conscience is transferred, a keystone is used to energize them and can give them commands or allow them to command themselves. Our golems are our ancestors."

The group sat quietly for a moment, processing everything Eridu said.

"Eridu, I thought dwarves didn't have the ability to use magic," Adalyn said.

"We don't."

"So, how is it possible then to create a golem if you can't do magic?"

"We have no innate ability to do magic, but we are quite skilled in manipulating things that have magical abilities. Our people have a deep connection to the earth and have found that different stones are able to conduct magical energy for different purposes. I really don't know the details, but I imagine those were used to create golems."

"So, the golems who traveled with the dwarves to Pieriun are asleep, and their keystones were stolen and brought back here. How do we know where to look for them?"

"We don't know exactly where the stolen keystones are, but that's not a problem, because keystones are interchangeable. They aren't made specifically for a certain golem. This book has a map of how to get to the sacred caves where dwarves become golems. There should be keystones we can use stored there."

Somehow, Adalyn had a feeling this wouldn't be as easy as it sounded.

After a quick breakfast the next morning, everyone helped break down camp, and the group started out toward the towering mountains. Each time they would begin to hear sounds that might be people, Eridu would pull out the map and reroute the group. Just when Adalyn's stomach started to grumble for lunch, they reached the base of the mountain and what looked like a cave.

"Don't tell me we have to go in there," groaned Vaeren.

Eridu looked over at him with a lifted brow. "Where else did you expect a dwarven smithy to be?"

"I'm tired of being underground," Vaeren grumbled, and Adalyn tried to hide her smirk as she entered the cave.

Eridu flipped open the book and turned to a new map while Venlian stepped up next to her, creating a glowing ball in his hand so she could see. "It looks like we should head to the right and continue down that way for a while. The keystones should be in one of the rooms near the end of this tunnel."

Adalyn's shoulders slumped a bit as she looked at the map and realized just how long the trail was that lay ahead of them.

The group trekked down the cavern paths for what felt like hours. Eventually, the stone walls appeared smoother and more squared. They passed heavy stone doors from time to time that became bigger, and carvings started to appear on them.

Eridu stopped suddenly in front of one. "I think this is it. They should be in here."

Looking the door over, Adalyn noticed it had runes and carvings of small beetles. A small keyhole caught her attention. "Don't tell me we need to find a key to get in."

The door groaned as Nolan gave it a shove. "Apparently, we don't."

Venlian stepped forward to help push the door open. The group followed into a room full of shelves of boxes.

Nolan glanced around the room. "Um, does anyone else find it odd that we didn't run into anyone on the way down here?"

"Maybe they were just somewhere else?" Vaeren suggested hopefully.

The door groaned again behind them, causing the group to turn around just as it closed. Venlian grasped at the latch to open the door, but it wouldn't budge. "Or maybe it's because their security measures are so good, they don't think they need to patrol these halls. Adalyn, can you try worldwalking back to the other side of the door?"

Closing her eyes, she focused on an image of the hall. Pain flared at the front of her head, and after a moment of trying without success, she opened her eyes. "I can't. It's as if something is blocking me."

"Well, of course there is. I would have been surprised if these walls hadn't been enchanted to stop people from just popping in and out of this room," Eridu scoffed. "We're dwarves, not children. They would have put security in place."

Vaeren groaned.

"Wait, the keyhole!" Adalyn exclaimed. "Maybe there's a key in here to let us back out."

"Possibly. It would have been smart to hide one in here just in case one of the dwarves who worked here locked himself in," Eridu said. "Why don't you all look for a key while Venlian and I find the keystones?"

The group separated and began searching. Venlian's comment about the dwarves depending on the cave's defenses seemed correct, because it wasn't long before he and Eridu found the keystones. They weren't hidden at all, but simply stored on the shelves. Venlian produced an enchanted bag, which somehow didn't seem to grow larger or heavier as they dumped box after box of keystones into it.

Reaching up on the top shelf, Adalyn pulled a box down to check inside and under it for the key, only to drop the box on her head and spill the contents everywhere.

"Seriously? There has to be an easier way to do this!" Getting down on the floor to pick up the items that had spilled, something went scuttling across the floor. "Eridu, do the dwarves have some sort of connection to beetles?"

"Not that I know of, why?"

"There were just a bunch of them carved onto the door, and there's one crawling around in here with us. I was just curious. Is there anything about it in that book you brought?"

Eridu stopped searching to flip through the book. "Beetles… beetles… hmm. Ah, here's something. Oh, that's not an ordinary beetle. It's a fire beetle. They're used to start the forges here. When scared or squished, they explode and catch anything around them on fire. These little bugs burn extra hot."

Adalyn looked around the room and noticed a few more of the beetles. "So, if we step on this beetle right now, it will cause a small explosion?"

"Well, according to this, the explosion wouldn't be small. It takes very high heat to start a dwarf forge. I would guess that if one of these beetles was scared or squished, this whole room would catch fire, and we would probably all die."

"That sounds fun. I vote for no bug stomping, then," Nolan piped up, then muttered, "never did like bugs."

Eridu chuckled. "I'm thinking not."

"I think I may have found something," Venlian said, gaining their attention. "It's a weighted lockbox. You have to have a specific weight put onto only one side of the balance in order to open the lock, but you normally only have four tries, or it locks itself shut for a predetermined amount of time."

"How long?"

"It's different for each one."

"So, what do we use for the weight? How do we know it's right?"

Venlian held out a box of stones. "This was on top of it, so I assume the unlocking weight is one of these."

Looking inside the box, Nolan counted twelve small stones. "They all look the same size to me. How are we going to figure out which is the correct one?"

"Let's do it in groups," Vaeren said. "If we weigh them in three groups of four each, we can eliminate which one weighs differently from the rest. That would be the stone to unlock the box."

Venlian nodded approvingly. "A wise suggestion. I agree."

The stones were divided, and the first two groups were put onto opposite sides of the scale. The scale remained level.

"That means the stone must be in the last group," Venlian said as he removed the stones from the scale. "All of the stones weighed the same between the two groups."

Adalyn put the last four stones onto the scale, placing two on each side. "Or it could mean they all weigh just a little bit off, and we got lucky."

"It could mean that, but I can't imagine the dwarves making this any harder for their own people to figure out than they had to."

Once the stones were in place, the scale tipped slightly to the right.

"So, it's one of the stones on the right?"

"Correct."

"Which one?"

Looking up, Adalyn saw Venlian furrow his brow, studying the scale. "I'm not sure, but we should be able to try each one and open the box. We have two tries left." He then reached over and took one stone off to move to the left. They heard a soft clicking sound as the stone sunk down and the box opened to reveal several levers, but the door didn't unlock.

"Could you hurry this up please, Venlian?" Vaeren asked, fidgeting with the hem of his coat.

Having been so engrossed in the scale, Adalyn realized that she hadn't looked around the room recently. There were beetles covering most of the floor and shelves, each of them crawling in through cracks in the walls.

"We need to hurry, or soon we won't be able to get to the door without blowing ourselves up in the process."

"Interesting," Eridu said as she studied the lockbox.

"What's interesting? It's a box with levers."

"This box appears to have been built into the room itself. It's a permanent fixture here. These levers are built into the floor and are probably connected to traps in the room as well as the lock on the door. If we don't pick the right lever, these beetles could be the least of our problems."

"Which one do we pick? Anyone notice anything that can help us figure this out?" Vaeren wiped sweat from his brow and took a deep breath. "I *really* want to get out of here."

While looking at the levers, Eridu quickly opened her book again. "I'm betting it's the one furthest from the door. See here? There's a set of runes etched into it at the base. It matches the ones on my map for this room specifically."

Adalyn added, "There were a set of runes on the door as well. I can't be sure, but these look familiar. Possibly the same ones?"

Venlian reached for the lever and pulled it toward the door. A soft clicking noise sounded in the room, but it was difficult to tell where it came from exactly. Vaeren rushed over to the door, tiptoeing around beetles, and tried to open it, but failed. Pale, he turned back with despair and desperation clearly etched on his face.

"Search for the source of the clicking. There was a keyhole in the door, and I'm hoping this click was the hiding spot for the key. Hurry, please, there are far too many beetles in here for my liking."

Adalyn looked around the room and noticed a stone in the floor to the right of the door that was raised ever so slightly. Going over to the stone, she pulled out a knife and tried to lever it up, but the stone would not give. Pushing the side furthest away from the door did nothing to move the stone. Neither did pushing the side toward the center of the room where she was crouched, or the side near the door. As she pushed the side toward the wall, the stone easily popped open, revealing a key hidden underneath.

"I found it! Let's get out of here."

The group quickly gathered around the door, stepping carefully around the fire beetles. Adalyn opened the door, and they all moved swiftly into the hallway as if afraid the door would close again with them still inside the room. Checking that they had everything, the group headed toward the entrance at double speed, with Vaeren setting the pace.

TEN

The time in the caves took most of the day, so the group set up camp in the forest nearby. Everyone kept the same routine as the night before, only Venlian joined Adalyn to forage for edible plants near the camp to fill out the group's meal.

"I wanted to thank you," Adalyn said tentatively while grabbing a mushroom from a moss-covered log.

Venlian bent to pick up a leafy bunch. "For what do I deserve thanks?"

"You saved me. Technically, you saved both me and Nolan."

"Ah, I assume the sword came in handy when you returned from your visit?"

"It most certainly did. How did you know?"

"How did I know to send you with the sword? Not those. Never those. Those will leave us all very sick for several days." His eyes followed her as Adalyn put the red-spotted mushrooms back on the ground and pointed at the cluster of orange-spotted ones next to them. "Yes, we can use those. About the sword, remember how I showed you the books in my library?"

"I do."

"After the first time you visited me in your dreams, I looked for your book and read parts of it out of curiosity. I didn't finish it, though."

Climbing over a grouping of green and blue boulders that almost seemed to glow in the setting sun, Adalyn stopped and turned back toward him. "Why did you stop?"

He locked eyes with her. "I saw that I was more than a mere mention in your story."

Not quite sure how to respond to that, she climbed down the other side of the boulders into a small grove with a stream running through it. "Is that a bad thing?"

"Not necessarily. It just means that our stories intermingle, and I didn't want to change our possible futures by attempting to interpret your story and my part in it."

"Is that why you forbade me from ever reading a living person's story? So it wouldn't change my actions and, as a result, the future?"

Bending before the creek to fill his flask with clean water, he answered without looking up, "It is." He stood, straightened his back, and started back towards camp. "We should return to the group before it gets dark. You never know what we will run into in these woods."

AFTER PULLING HER BEDROLL NEAR THE FIRE AS THE night grew cooler, Adalyn quickly fell asleep, exhausted by the day's events. Cooking in the kitchens and the training she had been doing with the sword master was physically taxing, but it hadn't prepared her for how fatigued she would be after hiking all day carrying everything she would need to survive.

Expecting to get a few hours of sleep before it was her turn for night watch, the unwelcome shaking of her shoulder, at what felt like immediately after her eyes had closed, made her want to cry. Maybe she wasn't cut out for this adventuring stuff. As exciting as it was, she preferred getting an uninterrupted night's sleep in a soft bed. Once she pried her eyes open, she noticed Eridu crouching down with a finger over her lips.

Adalyn cautiously crawled out of her bedroll and grabbed her blade, preparing for whatever had spooked their watchman. The group formed a circle around the camp, their backs to the fire, each taking a different direction to listen and watch for movement. It was silent. Not nighttime silent, where the nocturnal animals made their own sort of music, but dead silent.

"Put your weapons down and don't try anything stupid," a voice from Adalyn's left demanded of them.

Turning to look, she saw a human woman in black holding a sharp, curved blade to Eridu's throat. A strategic choice—Adalyn wondered how well that would have worked on Nolan or Venlian. Glancing over at the men across the camp from her, she watched as they slowly put their weapons down and did so as well, glancing from the woman to the forest around them. It wasn't until then that Adalyn noticed the shadows of over a dozen people inching closer. They were outnumbered, and very likely outmatched.

Venlian put his hands up as a sign of resignation. "We have no desire for any trouble. We are only a traveling group who stopped for rest. We did not know this land was claimed and unsafe to camp on. If you would be so kind as to free our friend, we will leave immediately."

The woman glanced around the group and looked at Venlian as if she had already made up her mind. "What kind of group travels with two humans, an elf, and a dwarf? Why are you on our land?"

"We are merely traveling as a group of friends to Merebrook, to attend a gathering at Zerdock Academy."

Adalyn was glad Venlian was doing all of the talking. She had no idea what she would have said if it had been up to her. She knew nothing of this place.

Removing the blade from Eridu's neck and stepping back, the woman stood tall as her crew emerged into the firelight. Venlian's story was believable, then. Adalyn would have to ask him another time about Zerdock Academy, and why humans, elves, and dwarves would travel there together.

"It's not safe in these woods," the woman said. "The war has forced creatures of all sorts out of their homes to seek new ones. We've found the remains of too many travelers over the last few years. Merebrook is three days away. Come rest in our village tonight where it's safe. We can help you gather your campsite and leave before drawing unwanted attention."

The group silently glanced at each other, all of their eyes eventually landing on Venlian. A graceful smile lit up his face. "We will take you up on your kind offer. I'm Venlian."

"Bevin. This is my crew. I'm sure you will get to know them at the village. Be quick now, and quiet."

Once finished, it didn't take long to reach Bevin's village. It reminded Adalyn a bit of her own, comprised of fewer than twenty buildings gathered together with a makeshift fence around the perimeter. Small gardens surrounded each brightly painted, wooden home. Even in the dark, the village seemed cheerful.

WAKING UP TO THE SMELL OF SIZZLING MEAT AND baked goods, and the feeling of Eridu's cold feet pressing against her calf, Adalyn groaned as the night before came crashing down on her. She was beyond grateful that Bevin had brought them to her home, or her parents' home, to be exact. Even though it was the middle of the night, the siblings were shuffled into other beds so that Adalyn and Eridu could share a bed in the girls' room. Venlian, Nolan, and Vaeren had been put up in the boys' room, and Adalyn smirked, wondering if any of them had made the choice to sleep in their bedrolls on the floor rather than share a bed.

Sitting up carefully so as to not wake up Eridu, she slipped on her shoes and tiptoed out the door and downstairs to the main room. Bevin's mother stirred something over the fire, adding to the sense of familiarity and home that the village had already implanted in Adalyn's mind.

"Good morning," Adalyn said, trying not to startle the woman. "Thank you for letting us stay in your home last night. The bed and safe space are greatly appreciated."

The curvy woman looked back at Adalyn and reached up to tuck a stray lock of hair back into her messy bun. "We are always happy to take in those who are in need. You're the first one up on this fine morning."

"It's a habit. I work in a kitchen, and I have to be one of the first up to have breakfast ready."

"Oh, where do you work? Perhaps I know it."

Adalyn froze for a moment, realizing that she might have just said too much. She couldn't let on that she wasn't from Chors without potentially bringing the army down on all of them.

"Currently, I'm not working anywhere. Perhaps I will find something once our traveling is done." Not an entire lie, considering that the castle had been ransacked, and who knew if she would ever work in the king's kitchen again. "I'm sorry, I didn't get your name last night. I'm Adalyn."

"Don't fret it, my dear. The name's Bella. Do you mind handing me that spoon right next to you?"

Reaching down to grab the spoon, Adalyn noticed just how much food Bella was cooking as she took in the room. Almost every flat surface was covered in varying stages of food preparation. Handing the spoon over, Adalyn asked, "Are you a baker or cook for the town?"

Bella laughed. "Oh, no! I don't have the spare time for that. Not with seven young'uns living at home still, and my husband gone for the war. Today, my daughter is gettin' married."

"Bevin? She didn't say anything last night."

The woman's laugh deepened. "Bevin? You thought I meant Bevin? I guess you don't know her well enough yet to know just how funny that really is. That girl's as wild as the curly mop on her head. No, my fourth child is getting married today. Bay's been in love with the boy since they were young'uns, and he turns seventeen tomorrow. They are getting married before he is drafted and leaves, just like all the other men in our village."

Adalyn hadn't considered what it was like for a normal family to live in a country at war. Pieriun had been at peace all her life, and the thought of drafting soldiers hadn't crossed her mind. Now that she thought about it, though, the entire group that had surrounded their campfire had been women and teenage boys.

"It's sad they are having to do it just before he leaves, but an exciting day for your family. I can help you with whatever you need this morning. It might be a bit before the rest of my group wakes up."

"Maybe not as long as you think." Bella nodded toward the stairs.

Nolan scratched his messy hair while stepping down the last few steps and froze when he saw the women watching him. "Um, good morning." He cleared his throat. "Do you have any water?"

Bella pointed to the sink and pump under the window. "Over there, dear. Cups are in the cupboard to the left."

"Thank you."

A noise behind her had Adalyn turning to watch as Venlian, followed by Eridu and then Vaeren, joined the trio in the increasingly shrinking main room.

Eridu looked around the room. "I see that you've been

busy this morning," she told Bella, then turned to Adalyn. "Already eaten?"

Bella lifted a ladle from a large pot on the stove, bringing it to her lips, then answered, "None of you have eaten yet, but I did make some marpleberry muffins and fried boar slices for you if you would like." She pointed to a pile of plates. "Help yourselves."

She continued addressing them as they did so, glancing at Venlian specifically, "If you aren't in a rush, you are all welcome to attend my daughter's wedding celebration tonight. The ceremony is only for immediate family, but the celebration is for everyone in the village." Her glancing became more frequent as she continued, fumbling with her hands. "I've heard it's good luck to have an elf at a wedding. Some sort of connection between a long life and a long, happy marriage. My family, our village, could use all the luck we can find."

Everyone in the room turned toward Venlian expectantly. If they really were a group of friends traveling to Zerdock Academy, would they be expected to stay? Would it destroy the safety that story brought if they refused? Adalyn held her breath, but Venlian looked unaffected by the strangeness of the request.

"We would love to stay today and celebrate with your family. Tomorrow morning, we will have to be on our way, though. We are expected."

Bella's smile melted Adalyn's heart as she turned to her. "If your offer to help with the cooking is still available, I could use some help this afternoon. I have everything under control for now, but if you come around for lunch, I can feed you and use your extra set of hands after."

"I am glad to be of service."

When they had finished their meal, Venlian turned toward Vaeren and Eridu. "Since we have a bit of free time, would you mind if we spoke? I would like to go over a few things with you." They nodded and followed him out the front door.

"I guess that leaves the two of us. Up for some practice? I might even let you win once or twice," Nolan asked, nudging Adalyn's shoulder with a big, goofy grin.

"Oh, is that a challenge I hear? I accept. Meet you in the field outside the main gate in five?"

"I'll be the one in layers of brown."

Bella coughed, catching the pair's attention. "About that—if you would like a change of clothes, I have some extras in the trunk under the stairs. Feel free to pick whatever fits. I can have my kids help wash what you're currently wearing so they are clean and dry by the time you leave tomorrow. If anything catches your interest to wear to the celebration tonight, feel free to pull it out and lay it on the beds you slept on."

Adalyn looked down and took a deep breath, smelling the sweat from the journey stuck to her with layers of dirt. "That would be greatly appreciated. Perhaps a bath before tonight, as well."

CHAPTER

ELEVEN

"Don't just stab at me randomly with your sword! I know you're better than that. Take this seriously, please."

Adalyn stepped forward, attempting to use proper form as Nolan barked formations at her, one after another. A quick swish and a push from him were all it took for her to end up on her back, completely out of breath. Her view of the clear, blue sky was blocked by his familiar figure, holding his sword in one hand while the other rested on his hip.

"What do you think of our hosts?" he asked.

"We haven't met most of them yet. I guess Bevin could be interesting to get to know, and Bella seems full of energy. You?"

"About the same. I wonder how Bevin ended up being in charge of the town guard. Self-designated, or was it a handed-down responsibility?"

"That's a good question. It would be interesting to find out. It broke my heart a bit when Bella told me her name this morning."

"Oh?"

"Made me think of Isabella, my friend in the kitchen. I don't know if she got out."

Nolan ran a hand over his face, then gave her a sympathetic look. "I understand. We really don't know anything about how the enemy works. Do they take prisoners? What are their rules of engagement? They are basically a complete mystery to us."

Adalyn didn't speak, fearing the tears she was holding back would let loose if she did.

Realizing that she wasn't about to get back up, Nolan laid on the grass next to her. "Do you ever miss living in a small town? You did live in one before working for Chef in the castle, didn't you?"

"I did, and I do… sometimes. It was quiet, but also oftentimes boring. Everyone knew everyone and watched out for each other the best that we could. In the summer, we had picnics along the river, then we celebrated the end of harvest in the fall with a bonfire, and in winter, we had sleigh rides and dances."

"Sounds nice."

"It was. Nothing compared to your life of adventure, though. Traveling constantly, meeting new people, and seeing new places."

"I loved it. Still do. As a kid, it was always exciting to visit different villages and towns, especially when they held celebrations and feasts for Queen Tillie. It's the kind of life I want my own children to have. Stability and adventure, all rolled into one."

Adalyn turned toward Nolan, studying his face as he

gazed up at the sky. "Do you have your own wagon in the caravan?"

"Nah, no need. It's just me. All of my siblings have married and moved out of my parents' wagon, so I crash there when I need to. Most of the time, I'm not with the caravan itself anymore. I'm typically scouting ahead. Gotten used to sleeping outdoors."

Her gaze shifted from his face to watch his chest instead as it steadily rose and fell with each breath. "What about when you start your own family?"

Nolan's face took on a faint flush. "I would get my own wagon then for my family." Rolling onto his side, he asked, "Could you ever live a nomadic life with a wagon full of kids?"

It was Adalyn's turn to blush. "I'm not sure. I never considered it before."

Nodding and rolling onto his back, Nolan returned his gaze to the sky. "Maybe you should."

Frozen for a moment, she shook herself and got up. "I should go. I promised Bella I would be back to help her prepare for the wedding. See you then." Gathering her things, she rushed into the village without looking back, afraid of just how readable her face would be.

Back at the house, the main room was packed with women of varying ages, hustling while carrying an array of bowls and other instruments. Dodging a girl of about nine who was carrying an especially stinky block of cheese, Adalyn bumped into a bowl, knocking it into several others. The loud crashing sound alerted the entire room to her presence.

"You're back! I could use someone with professional

experience to help us pull this together." Bella waved Adalyn over. "Come help me over here. What was your specialty in the kitchens you were in?"

"A little bit of everything."

"Ah, well, let's start you out by chopping the myre root with Bevin so that the greenlie moss will rise."

"I'm sorry, myre root? Greenlie moss?"

"Unfamiliar with them?" Bella chuckles. "What kind of kitchen were you in that didn't use those? Probably some fancy one where these come to you already processed. Myre root has sugar in it that, when combined with the particular fungi in greenlie moss, will help bread rise without any aftertaste. Some folks dry both of them and sell them in powdered forms. Too much extra work for a busy woman like me, though. We go with the originals."

Blank-faced, Adalyn turned toward the table where Bevin sat with a glint in her eye. She waved her over and handed her a knife. "Here, I'll show you. You certainly aren't from around these parts. Sorry about the scare last night, by the way."

Picking up the knife, Adalyn began chopping, copying what Bevin did with the unfamiliar plant, trimming the fine fern-like top off of the purple bulb and chopping it into tiny pieces. "I don't mind. I appreciate having a safe place to sleep and a bed for a night."

"Still, I know I was rough. Ma said she told you about all of the men in our village being gone. I have to stay strict with the few left here to protect our village. Especially if I ever want to leave."

"Leave? Where do you want to go?"

"I want to volunteer for the guard. I know women aren't generally allowed to go to the front lines, but I've heard rumors of women volunteering and being accepted. Still, I can't do that until I have a replacement trained."

Adalyn didn't know what to say. Even Pieriun didn't have many women in their ranks. There were certain roles most women were allowed and expected to be in. Those who went outside of those roles typically had to give up having a family or any committed relationships.

"Don't mind me. I'm a bit of an oddball, I know," Bevin continued. "Let's try to finish up here so we can get ready for the wedding. The women in town are abuzz that there will be a few new men to dance with this evening."

A dry laugh escaped her, as Adalyn had a feeling those men had no idea what they were in for.

BELLA'S "TRUNK" TURNED OUT TO BE SEVERAL trunks, all filled with odds and ends and a variety of clothing in different sizes. Adalyn assumed they were hand-me-downs waiting for their next owner to grow into them. Unsure what exactly the people of this village wore to a wedding celebration, she asked Bevin for help picking something out.

The dress they picked was a beautiful dark blue with fitted sleeves that ended just below the elbow, and a high neck with a slit down to the top of her corset. Laced up the back, it was snug to her hips and eventually flared out until it touched the ground. A lot of love had obviously been put into the dress, with red, pink, and gold flowers embroidered up the skirt and along the cuffs, intertwined with green ivy and leaves. Adalyn was sure she had never worn anything so beautiful in her life.

After Eridu laced up her dress, Adalyn turned to return the favor. "I can't believe that they have a neighbor with a dress that fits me!" Eridu repeated for the umpteenth time.

"Didn't they say this neighbor's grandmother was a dwarf from the mountain we were in yesterday?"

"Yes, isn't that interesting? Can you imagine a dwarf deciding to marry a human and move away from her home under the mountain? It's practically unheard of!"

Adalyn moved over to the mirror, picking up locks of her hair and trying to decide what to do with it. "Why is that?" A look of embarrassment etched into the reflection of Eridu's face made her pause.

"It's going to sound silly, but dwarves live their entire lives under the mountains. A few used to go out to trade, but never traveled far from home. Old wives' tales claim that if you leave the mountain and do something wrong, you will fall into the sky." She shrugged, and a small smile spread on her face. "At least under the mountain, you have a rock ceiling to bump into and can try again."

Today was full of things to which Adalyn didn't know quite how to respond. "Do you believe that?"

Eridu shuffled her feet. "I'm not sure. I can honestly tell you that stepping out of that gate into this world was the scariest thing I've ever done."

"I didn't realize. You had never been out of the caves, had you?"

"None of us have for generations. We couldn't risk being seen."

Adalyn turned toward Eridu and reached out to grab her hand. "Thank you for being so brave. You have been invaluable on this journey." The two smiled at each other, and then Adalyn took a deep breath. "Any ideas for what to do with this mess on my head? I've never been any good at styling."

Eridu's face lit up even more. "Sit and let me do it for you. I'm sure we can figure something out from styles I've seen in a few old books. If nothing else, it will be fun to try!"

TWELVE

Carrying a large tray filled with greens and blossoms she couldn't identify, Adalyn followed the women from the village who had arrived to bring the food to the wedding site. With the family gone for the ceremony, she thought it sweet that the village was helping set up the celebration. They had left the boundaries of the village a few minutes ago and were heading uphill on a well-worn path into the forest. Lightning bugs flitted around them, giving the forest a magical glow.

As they entered a clearing, ruins of a large, stone building came into view. Candles were lit on outcrops of crumbling stone and surrounded by flowers on tables spread throughout the ruins and surrounding forest.

Following the women, Adalyn set down her tray and took in the scene. It was unlike anything she had ever seen before. Sure, the village was similar to her own, but this wasn't. In the capital, and even in the small village where she grew up, all weddings she had attended were either at a church or someone's home.

Eridu joined her and spun, allowing her skirt to swirl around her, ending the twirl in a slight curtsy. "I don't think I have ever felt so much like a girl. I've read of these kinds of dresses and weddings, but never thought I would get to see one."

The red dress suited Eridu, highlighting the blush in her cheeks and the red tones in her hair. The embroidery around the neck and sleeves showed a mix of dwarven and human influence, with sinuous flowers and vines mixed with geometric blocks.

"You look absolutely beautiful. I have to admit, this is pretty magical."

Adalyn noticed Vaeren, Nolan, and Venlian entering the ruins. All three of them were dressed in sturdy, fitted jackets with matching pants. Nolan's clothes were forest green, Vaeren's were a dark purple, and Venlian's ice blue. Adalyn couldn't help but admire how this village seemed to love color and celebrate every aspect of their lives with it.

Seeing Adalyn, Nolan waved, a smile lighting up his face. Venlian had a small smile of his own when he saw the women. Music played, and the men joined them to watch as the celebration began.

The crumbling entrance of the ruined building was soon filled with the family of the wedded as they danced through it and greeted everyone with smiles and waves. After a quick announcement, the happy couple followed and stopped in the center of the crowd to greet and acknowledge their guests.

When the groom waved, the crowd quieted. "We want to thank everyone for coming out to celebrate this special day with us. It is difficult that many are unable to join us, but when they hear of this happy union, I am sure they will celebrate for us as well."

"Everything looks beautiful. We couldn't have done this without you," the bride added. Then she sidestepped into a small curtsy, flaring her white dress, which was adorned with vibrant flowers. "Patsy McClude, the flowers from your garden that were stitched onto this dress are the most beautiful I have ever beheld. For that, we would like to start the dances for you and the incredibly talented individuals who made our wedding outfits."

The music started back up, and a group of women joined the bride and groom, dancing to a lively jig together. A few moments later, the rest of the crowd joined in, dancing in a circle around the group. When the song was over, the bride and groom took turns thanking different people for everything that had been done for their wedding, calling them up and dancing with them while the rest of the guests danced around them in celebration and thanks as well.

When those who helped with food were called up, Adalyn didn't know what to do. She wasn't sure if she should go. Was she supposed to do a specific dance that she couldn't possibly know?

"Come join us!" Bevin called, dancing through the crowd to Adalyn. "This is celebrating you, as well."

Bevin grabbed her hand and turned, pulling Adalyn into the center of the crowd. Turning to face her, Bevin threw her hands in the air and bounced back and forth on the balls of her feet, spinning occasionally. Adalyn tentatively swayed back and forth, unfamiliar with this kind of music and dancing. Curly hair bounced around her shoulders and into her face, and then Bevin grabbed her hands again and danced with her in a circle. Eventually, Adalyn let go and joined the crowd, closing her eyes as she moved however the music took her.

Once the music stopped, everyone turned toward the musicians and clapped, catching their breaths. Looking around, Adalyn saw her companions had found a table, where they now sat. The crowd dispersed to find their own places as well, most detouring to the food tables first and going to their seats with full plates and glasses.

Deciding to wait before getting food herself, Adalyn wound her way to her group. "I see you have made yourselves at home."

"Do you blame us? Just watching you was exhausting. Plus, when Sarah invited us to grab food with her and sit down, we figured we may as well miss the rush. It appears to have been a good idea. Oh!" Eridu pointed to a young woman with ashy hair sitting next to her. "By the way, this is Sarah. She is the one who loaned me the dress."

"So, you're the girl I've heard so much about," Sarah said with a wide smile. "It's a pleasure to meet you."

A dwarf grandmother, indeed. She was almost as short as Eridu!

Adalyn smiled at the woman in return and nodded. "And I, you. I do need to find something to drink, though."

"No need, take the empty seat. Nolan grabbed some

food and a drink for you when he was going through the line," Eridu informed her with a wink,

Nolan blushed. "It was no big deal. I just thought, since I was going through already, that I might get you started."

Taking the seat next to him, she nudged his shoulder. "It's very much appreciated." Turning toward Sarah and gesturing to their surroundings, she continued, "This place is enchanting. Does your village commonly have weddings here?"

A look Adalyn couldn't decipher passed over Sarah's face. "This is the first wedding we've done here since it looked like this. This was… well, *is*, our church. Our village is fairly close to a gateway, and during a skirmish, our chapel was destroyed."

The group shared a look with each other. The gateway Sarah mentioned was probably the same one they'd come through.

"I'm so sorry to hear that," Eridu responded.

"A fact of war. You're never entirely safe. The soldiers from Pieriun holed up inside the chapel while waiting for reinforcements, and our soldiers took them out. At least we won that battle. I've heard stories of villages and towns that have been taken over by Pieriun soldiers and the tortures they've been put through."

The thought hadn't crossed Adalyn's mind that soldiers from her world had taken over parts of Chors in the Great War. Was it possible they could run into Pieriun soldiers who didn't know them and could cause problems for their small group? But why were the soldiers still here, still fighting? That was centuries ago. When Bevin had mentioned there was a war going on, Adalyn had assumed Chors was fighting with a different enemy. She wanted to ask Sarah, but worried that doing so would expose them and cause more harm than good.

Adalyn realized Nolan was talking to her and shook herself from her thoughts. "Sorry, what did you say?"

"I was asking if you wanted to dance."

"I didn't know you could dance."

His face lit up. "The queen's caravan is known for our love of dancing."

Intrigued, she held out her hand in acceptance, and he whisked her away into the dancing crowd. Before, she had felt connected to the mass of dancers around her, but this time, she couldn't take her eyes off of Nolan. The men she had seen dancing at court, the few times she'd taken food up for a ball, had been stiff. The dances there were structured and choreographed. The people of Chors, in contrast, danced erratically and free. Nolan was somehow different. When he moved, everything seemed controlled and perfect, yet unexpected.

His eyes closed as he felt the music, only to reopen and connect with hers immediately. His look of pure joy encouraged her to move to the music with no self-judgment.

As the song ended, the two joined the claps of the crowd, and the musicians began to play a slower tune. Adalyn took a step to return to her seat, only to be stopped by Nolan pulling her to his chest and resting one hand on her hip while holding one of hers with the other.

"Just one more."

His soft eyes, asking her to stay in their own way,

melted her a little inside. She smiled and nodded, closing her eyes as they swayed with the music. Each step brought them a little bit closer until only their clothing separated their bodies.

"You look beautiful tonight."

"Thank you. This dress is truly something else."

He brushed a stray hair from her face and tucked it behind her ear. "True, the dress is stunning. You really make it stand out, though."

She tucked her head against his chest to hide the blush of her cheeks and smile on her face, unsure what exactly to say in response that wouldn't sound silly or childish. The flush only deepened, and her grin grew bigger when she felt the weight of his head resting against hers. The two finished the song in comfortable silence, enjoying the embrace, and took an extra moment to untangle from their position after the song ended.

He cleared his throat and glanced toward the food table. "Um, I'm going to grab another drink. Do you want anything?"

"I'm fine, thank you." She watched as he left, wondering if her feelings were simply from the moment they'd just shared, or something more. Hearing the band start another upbeat song, she moved to the edge to watch the crowd enjoying the celebration.

The smiles of the people dressed in all their finery made Adalyn's heart ache for Isabella. She would have loved this. Adalyn could almost hear her chattering away next to her over the food and the lights and how beautiful everything was.

Adalyn jumped at the sound of something like glass

breaking just behind her. Before she could turn around to see what happened, it happened again to her left. Soon, the sound of shattering sounded all around her. Confused, she realized that everyone was breaking their dishes as they finished eating. Strange; it seemed like a waste of good dishes.

With no one she knew near enough to ask what was happening, she decided to meander around and stretch her legs, taking note of individuals gathering the pieces and carrying them outside the ruins. Curious, Adalyn followed, finding a group of people bent over a small pool of water in a very tiny creek. They had baskets of broken dishes piled around them and were dunking the pieces in the water, then speaking over them.

"It's a unique tradition, one I never expected to see in person." Venlian said, making Adalyn jump.

"What are they doing?"

"They are fixing the broken plates."

Intrigued, she stood in silence with him, watching the plates be dipped in the water. The pieces matched with their mates and a small but bright golden glow ran along the seam, sealing them together.

Venlian picked up a repaired plate and moved it around to show a slight glistening in the repaired cracks. "That water has fine minerals and trace amounts of magic in it. They attach together with only a very faint, pearlescent crack at the seal. Essentially, they are magically gluing the dishes back together."

"Can it be done repeatedly?" Adalyn asked. "It seems that the dishes would become broken beyond repair if they did this at every wedding."

"They use a new set for each one. Did you notice that people were using different dishes? Some had large plates, some small, others used bowls. That's because this set will be given to the bride and groom to use. It's to remind them of the vows they made today and that when things become broken, such as in a fight, you have to put the pieces back together and move forward, to enjoy the beauty of the relationship after you've gone through the trials."

"That has to be one of the sweetest things I've ever heard."

"Chors has its charms."

The pair stood by and watched as the group continued to piece the dishes back together, a peaceful calm settling between them.

Eridu's voice snapped Adalyn out of her daze, "Adalyn? Venlian? I'm going to head back to the house and try to get some sleep. Are we still heading out first thing in the morning?"

"We are," Adalyn replied, turning toward her friend. "Let me walk back with you. I could use some rest before our push for home." The girls left Venlian, who continued to watch the repairing of the dishes with a look of curiosity and respect.

THIRTEEN

Upon their return, they stepped through the gate to find dwarven and human guards with swords and arrows pointing at them. A dwarf near Venlian held up a hand. "At ease, men. This is our group returning home. I hope you were successful."

"We were. Did they give you orders on where to send us when we returned?" Venlian asked.

"No, sir. You've been gone for so long that we were sure you were lost."

Adalyn found that odd. "We were only gone for three, almost four, days. It wasn't that long."

The soldiers glanced at each other, and the leader responded, "You've been gone for over six weeks."

This time, it was her small group who exchanged worried glances. Venlian stepped toward the pathway. "That doesn't make sense. If that is the case, I think it wise for me to report to the two kings and queens sooner rather than later. I'm going to see them now. We can speculate about the time difference after. The rest of you should get some rest. I will let you know what I find out."

After exiting the tunnel leading to the gateway, Adalyn watched the group split up. Venlian and Vaeren headed toward the dwarven king's palace, Nolan toward his group's camp, and Eridu assumedly toward her home.

Adalyn had been thinking about worldwalking and the Banneret as they'd walked from the village to the gateway, and an idea had struck her. If there was a common area for the Banneret, there had to be a dormitory as well somewhere near it. Finding herself free for the moment, she decided to explore. Making her way back through the ruined city and up the passage, she opened the door to the common room, only to find a familiar face.

"I wondered if you were ever going to make it back here," Glenda said, lounging on a sofa. "I thought you might have met your end in Chors."

"Not quite. It is odd, though—there's a time difference between here and Chors. We were only in Chors for a few days, but apparently, we've been gone longer than that."

"*Much* longer. Hmm, I wonder… You know what, never mind. Let me think about it and get back to you. It's good to see you."

"Likewise. You might be able to help me. I had the thought that, if the Banneret lived down here and have this common room, there should be rooms where they slept."

"Of course! I can show you to the dorms. You could even have my old room, if you want. First, sit down. Let's chat. Was your expedition a success? I'm also curious if you had the opportunity to use your ability while you were there."

Adalyn sat on a faded red armchair, which released a plume of dust, forcing a cough out of her. "I did try once. I was in a room in the dwarven tunnels under a mountain, but it didn't work. Eridu thought it was possibly because the stone was enchanted. We found the keystones there and brought them back."

Glenda nodded. "I agree with Eridu about the stone hampering your ability. The dwarves have always been able to do some incredible stuff with enchantments. Of course, thanks to your expedition, you will soon see one of the most miraculous things they have done. Now, tell me from the beginning about coming into your worldwalking ability. Did you experiment with it much before meeting me down here?"

Adalyn explained about having strange dreams and restless nights, then the incident in the kitchen and the strange gathering in the forest. She told Glenda about Venlian taking her to his library and how she'd learned that her dreams were actually worldwalking, then been given the sword and key.

"I'm sure Venlian understands the ability to a degree, but having someone who has the same ability may be a bit more beneficial." Chuckling to herself and shaking her head, Glenda mumbled, "He always was a bit of a know it all."

Adalyn jumped forward in her seat. "I would love to be trained by you!"

"Ah… I wouldn't necessarily call it training. A lot of it you will have to figure out on your own. The ability really changes with each individual. I would say that I can be a guide or mentor rather than a trainer."

"That's fair. When can we start?"

"How about right now? Tell me, what do you see in this room?"

Taking a moment to look, Adalyn began listing the items she saw. "Obviously, there's you and me. Lots of books and bookshelves. A dining table and fireplace…"

"Focus on me for a second. What is different to you about me compared to everything else in this room?"

Adalyn thought for a moment. "You glow?"

Glenda snorted. "Try again."

"I guess you're not really here. I mean, you are, but you're a spirit, I think. I can see the furniture you're on through you."

"Exactly. I'm currently using my ability to pull myself between my plane and yours."

"What do you mean by plane?"

"It's difficult to understand with words. Let me show you instead. I'm going to stay right here but move to my world. Follow me with your ability. Feel the shift in my presence."

Glenda started to disappear before Adalyn's eyes, causing her to panic. "Wait! I can't see you anymore!"

Reappearing, Glenda gave her a knowing look before she began to fade out again.

Throwing her head back and huffing, Adalyn grumbled, "I still don't get it."

Glenda's disembodied voice spoke from the fireplace, "Come find me."

Adalyn peeled herself from her seat and walked over to

the fireplace, her arms outstretched and flailing as she tried to feel Glenda's whereabouts.

Hearing laughter from the opposite corner, Adalyn quickly turned around and hurried to stand next to a small table and chairs. She reached out with her hands again, feeling the seats individually only to find them empty.

The laughing intensified, and Adalyn followed the sound with her eyes as it moved around the room. "Will you just stop and show yourself to me?"

Silence filled the room for a few moments. "The fact that you can hear me means that you have partially world-walked into the realm I am in. Close your eyes, take a deep breath, and then open them and try to find me again."

Adalyn followed the instructions and closed her eyes. Taking a deep breath, she grounded herself in the room and tried to take in every detail in her mind like she had when escaping the cell, then opened her eyes.

To her amazement, there were other spirits in the room. Some played games or read books, while others watched them with interest. "Why couldn't I see everyone before?"

"We live on a different plane now. We are with you and live within the same confines, but it's not the same. No one else can see us or feel us."

"Wait, you were a Banneret. How are you here? Is this the afterlife?" A memory of being pulled into her spirit form and watching spirits come out of the archway in the forest came to mind. "No, that's not right. The spirits I saw come out of the arch... No, not an arch. A gateway. Were you in that?"

"I was. It was part of the spell. Someone has broken the living spell cast on the gates. We were set free, or at least, free of the gates."

The image of Nightshade and the cloaked men popped into Adalyn's head. "This is a lot to take in. Are you ghosts?"

"I don't think so. I don't feel dead. I certainly thought I was dying when we cast the spell, though."

"So you are spirits, but not dead. Living normal lives? Until when?"

"We have no idea, and to be honest, it's really boring being a spirit. With effort, we can interact physically with some things, but not everything. Food, for instance. Sure, I can touch it, and even put my mouth around it, but I can't taste anything."

"I am so sorry. Food is one of my greatest joys in life. I could see how that would be disheartening."

Glenda slowly nodded with a truly downtrodden look. "We don't know why we're stuck here like this, or for how long. At least we are no longer alone. The spirits have been traveling to the places where they used to live, so the Banneret have been gathering here. Word has spread that there is a worldwalker who might be able to help."

"What? That's a bit much… I don't know how to help. I can barely use my ability." Adalyn tried to take a deep breath as panic grabbed hold of her. "I'm not important. I can't fix other people's problems. I just want to live a quiet life."

Taking her hand, Glenda tried to calm her. "It's all right. We will figure it out. We just need time. I've learned that our ability is one that tends to be useful for finding solutions to strange problems. You'll see. Let's go find you a bed and linens that aren't dusty so you can get some rest. I have something I need to show you when you're ready."

Taking another deep breath to calm her nerves, Adalyn nodded without looking at Glenda. "You can show me now."

"No, not right now. You look exhausted, and this will require you to figure out another worldwalking skill. Rest first. What I have to show you shouldn't be going anywhere."

FOURTEEN

Sleeping underground was an odd experience for Adalyn. She'd gotten used to the busyness of the castle, where someone was always about. Alone in the Banneret dormitory, she'd slept great. It was truly dark and quiet, and the room didn't feel too creepy once she removed the several inches of dust and dug some moth-eaten blankets out of a chest.

It was waking up that was odd, with no light of any kind. She had no idea what time it was, or how long she had slept.

Putting her shoes back on, she made a mental note to grab some decent blankets and a pillow when she was in the dwarves' new city.

After throwing on her coat, she headed back to the common room to see what Glenda wanted to show her before returning to the dwarves in search of food. In an attempt to practice her newfound skill, she opened her senses, greeting the spirits she encountered along the way with a smile and a nod, shocking a few of them.

The common room was even more crowded than it had been before, and it took Adalyn a moment of searching to find Glenda in a corner of the room, arguing over a game of chess with a stocky man sporting the largest and reddest beard she had ever seen.

"That's an illegal move and you know it!" The bearded man slammed his fist on the table, causing the pieces to jump.

Glenda leaned back casually in her chair with a sly grin. "Oh, Ardent, dear, you wouldn't think that was an illegal move if you actually knew the rules to the game. You don't even know how to move half of your pieces. Now, no fair being a poor sport and destroying the placement on the board."

The man glared at her, his face turning redder by the second.

Adalyn coughed.

Both of them looked up at her. "Ah, you've finally woken up," Glenda remarked. "I hope you rested well."

"Very well, thank you. Am I interrupting anything?"

"Nothing that I mind being interrupted," the man harrumphed.

"Someone doesn't like losing. Do we, big guy?" Glenda taunted.

Ardent stood. "I don't mind losing when it's a fair loss. You're a sneaky one, Glenda. I will take my leave and see you ladies later. I need a break from being beaten so badly over and over again."

Glenda watched him leave and gestured toward his empty chair. "Really, he is a good man. Better than I let on. Someone has to keep him humble, though. He was one of my fellow Banneret for quite some time. Left the post to take care of his sick wife."

"He sounds like a good man. I hope to see him around more."

"I'm sure you will. He tends to show up when he's needed. Now, how are you feeling? Ready for some more mentoring?"

"Yes. I'm excited!"

"Good. This may be a little more difficult than yesterday because it's not as easy to show, but you've technically done this already without trying. We are going to work on separating your spirit from your body."

While Venlian had said that she'd done this frequently in her sleep, the memory of her spirit slamming back into her body the two times she could remember it had Adalyn letting out an unintentional groan.

"Can you teach me how to do it so that it doesn't hurt?"

Glenda looked at her, confused. "What do you mean, hurt? This shouldn't ever hurt."

"I remember doing this twice. Once when I saw the spirits coming out of the gateway, and once when Venlian showed me the library. Both times, it was pretty painful being pulled back to my body."

"Ah, I think I understand now. Both times, you were not traveling of your own free will. I have a feeling that when the living spell on the gateways was broken, the gates called all free spirits. It would only make sense that it would have called your spirit as well, since you don't know how to prevent something from tearing your spirit from your body. I can teach you that later, but for now, keep your sword on you at all times. Part of the enchantments on it are defenses against such things."

"That makes sense. I guess Venlian called me to give me the sword and the key, so I wasn't in control of that one, either. That's kind of scary, actually. The sword is truly enough to prevent that?"

"It will be for now. Let's go ahead and begin. I think you are going to want to see what I have to show you."

Several frustrating minutes later, Adalyn followed Glenda down the halls back toward the castle in her spirit form, having finally found success in leaving her body behind in the chair.

Instead of working their way back to the entrance in the kitchen that Adalyn knew about, Glenda turned down paths that led deeper underground. The halls became shorter and narrower the further they went, until they reached what appeared to be a dead end.

"Are we lost?"

"No, we're not lost. The magic on this door hasn't faded. Because it was made to look like just another wall, it was forgotten and left alone. We are spirits, though. Doors and walls mean nothing to you in this form. Walk through it."

Adalyn played with the cuffs of her coat, staring at the wall of stone before her. "What if it's not actually a door? How long of walking through solid stone before I should turn around? Can I get lost or stuck that way?"

Glenda chuckled. "It's not possible for you to get stuck. There is a door there. It will only take a moment to walk through to the other side."

Releasing her sleeves and taking a deep breath,

Adalyn stepped forward. There was a moment of darkness as she passed through the stone, and then she was standing in another hallway, a set of stairs leading up before her.

Glenda appeared next to her. "I told you that you would be fine."

"One of these days, you're going to have to tell me why I can walk on the floor and feel it under me as a spirit, but somehow also walk through doors and walls."

"It's all in the mind. You can go through the floor and ceiling as well if you would like. Really, we are walking because it's what your mind understands for movement. We can just float along if you prefer."

"Depending on how long these stairs go, I just may take you up on that suggestion."

The well-worn stairs would have been tricky to walk up if they had been in their bodies. The edges were smoothed, and deep indents in the stone would have made it difficult to keep their footing.

"The Banneret have been scouting around the castle and city while you were gone," Glenda said. "It passes the time and makes us feel useful. We've learned much that will help in the coming battle to retake the kingdom. Kings Coeus and Thanmog sent some soldiers on scouting missions as well, but they're physically limited by their bodies in a way that we are not."

Soon, Glenda led her through several locked doors and gates until they entered a small room with two men in it.

Adalyn froze.

"You needn't be afraid. They don't know you're here. They can't even sense you," Glenda reminded her as she walked confidently through the room and another locked door.

Following behind, Adalyn stopped suddenly as the realization of where she was dawned on her. "You brought me to the dungeon. The cells haven't been used in forever."

"They are occupied now. Unfortunately, by inhabitants of the city and castle who couldn't escape. That's not all I wanted to show you, though. Follow me."

Adalyn's heart broke as she walked past cell after cell. All were filled with a large number of people who shared a starved and empty-eyed look.

Glenda stopped and turned toward one cell on their left specifically. As Adalyn joined her and looked in, an inferno ignited inside of her.

"Isabella! No!"

"Remember, she doesn't know you're here."

Rushing into the cell, Adalyn stood next to her best friend, tears rolling down her face and fists clenched as she tried to control her anger. "I have to get her out! How can I do that? I'm sure I can transport things with me with this ability. If it takes my clothes and items with me, I know I've got to be able to bring living things, too."

"You can. Just not here. The dungeons are enchanted to prevent it, like the dwarven room under the mountain. It's why I had to bring you here as a spirit."

"How did you know she was here? To even look for her? You've never met her."

"I sensed you after I was released from the spell and followed you back to the kitchen. I trailed you for quite a while, hoping you would sense me. When you were gone for so long on your expedition, I thought I should come and see what the Chors army was doing and found her."

Adalyn reached her arms out to try and grab Isabella, only for them to go right through her. "I have to make this work. She can't stay here!"

Glenda shook her head with pity in her eyes. "You can't. Not yet. I wanted you to know that she is here and alive. Later, after you've had some food and rested again, we can train on how to transport someone with you. When the opportunity arrives, you can strike and save your friend."

Adalyn knew Glenda was right and hated it. There was nothing she could do for Isabella right now. Wiping away tears and feeling defeated, she quietly questioned her mentor, "You said you've scouted. Show me what you've found. Maybe I can be of some use to help speed things up and get her out of here sooner."

"I like how you think," Glenda replied. "Come along. There's a lot to see."

WITH SOME GUIDANCE, RETURNING HER SPIRIT TO her body was easy and painless. Adalyn still wasn't sure she would ever get used to the adjustment of how her senses were different between the two. Her vision changed, and the lack of ability to sense air or even have the need to breathe while in her spirit form felt wrong.

After some stretching of her limbs and a quick good-bye, Adalyn worked her way back toward the dwarven dwellings. Hunger was overriding her exhaustion from the use of her ability, and she needed to tell the king everything she had learned while it was fresh on her mind.

Hurrying through the old ruins, she paused when a familiar shade of pale hair appeared over a crumbling wall. Curiosity piqued, she decided her hunger could hold for another few minutes and chose to join him.

"What are you doing?"

"I'm remembering things that are lost," Venlian replied without moving. "This city was truly a sight to behold back in the day—one of the largest I personally have ever encountered. It's sad to think of everyone who was lost because of pride and fear." Finally looking at her, he tilted his head a little. "You look like you got some rest. Where did you go? I looked for you but couldn't find you."

"Sorry about disappearing like that. I discovered the Banneret's dormitory and stayed there. I'm looking for some food right now, if you want to join me."

"I have some time before my next meeting begins."

"Is that meeting, by any chance, with the two kings and queens?"

"It is. Why do you ask?"

"Could I tag along? I've got some information that I think they will want to hear."

Venlian gave her a quizzical look. "You do?"

"I do. I've been with Glenda, and she's shown me many things the Banneret have learned while we've been away. It would be better if I delivered it in person."

Without looking away, he gestured toward the new city. "Then I suggest we hurry and find food so as not to be late. Lead the way."

Beginning their trek up the old streets, thoughts of the

living spell and the spirits wandering around weighed heavy on Adalyn's mind. "Venlian, when you were here before, did you participate in preparing the spell that ended the war? I'm assuming you didn't participate in casting it, since you're still here. Do elves have that kind of magic?"

"I did not participate. The king was growing more and more unstable as the war waged on, and I realized there would be no honorable end to it. My suggestions were ignored, and some very troubling decisions were made."

"That doesn't answer my question about elves."

"We prefer not to talk about our abilities."

"So, you have some."

"I do, just not magic in the sense that you are thinking. Elves are not wizards or sorceresses. We all have our own subtle abilities."

Adalyn got the sense that he wasn't willing to give up what his were yet, so she decided to move on for now. "How did the spell come about? Did the king have powers of his own?"

"He did not. At least, none that I ever saw. Initially, he was fascinated by magic, though, and had a private library of books on the subject. I don't think the king I met when I first came here would have considered the spell he cast. He truly was driven mad by the pressure of everything. His daughter didn't help."

"So, he found or invented a spell to end the war. Did you know what the spell was supposed to do?"

"When I left, the details of what would happen when the spell was cast weren't given. Only that it could end the war and would take the sacrifice of every magic-possessing individual to work."

"So, they knew it would kill everyone involved? That's crazy. It would be impossible to get everyone on board with that."

"Not as impossible as you might think. It took an incredible amount of power, but he convinced most of the council that it was the only way they could win. All of the Banneret and a huge number of other magic-possessing humans, dwarves, and elves committed themselves to casting the spell. I worried that it would cost them their lives. It was a big part of my decision to leave."

Remembering the spirits at the gateway and in the Banneret common room, Adalyn wondered, "Do you think those who gave their lives to cast this spell could possibly be alive within it?"

Venlian gave her a quizzical look. "You speak of a living spell, one which would bind a being's spirit with their magical essence. That would enable them to live and think within a spell. This is an idea that has been a favorite topic of discussion for elves for centuries, but it has never been proven. Why do you ask?"

An image of her ghostly mentor came to mind as ideas flitted around in her head. Not fully understanding yet, Adalyn chose to keep her thoughts to herself for the moment. "No particular reason." After a moment of silence, she blurted out, "If someone was trapped in the spell and the spell was broken, would they still be around?"

"No. If it was broken, they would be free."

Adalyn fidgeted with the hem of her sleeve and looked

away as they walked. "Hypothetically, if their spirits were still around, what would that mean?"

Venlian stopped walking and waited for her to look at him. "That would mean that the spell wasn't entirely broken, hypothetically speaking. Like I said, I haven't found any actual examples of this happening in the records. Are you sure you don't want to tell me anything?"

Adalyn sighed. "I just don't understand it all, so it makes me hesitant to share my thoughts."

"Ah, I see. I have learned over the years that discussing our questions can help us understand them better and reach conclusions faster," Venlian said.

Searching his face, Adalyn saw only open kindness, no frustration or condescension. Her confidence buoyed, she shared what Glenda had told her about the spell as they continued on. They discussed the implications over a simple meal.

"I am in awe that King Dragmire found a way to successfully complete a living spell, and such a large one at that," Venlian said. "Based on what you saw and Glenda has shared, Nightshade and the cloaked men in the forest must have indeed found a gateway, and were successful in opening them, which partially broke the living spell. That released the spirits who were involved in casting it. But the fact that the spirits are wandering indicates that they aren't entirely free of it, so some part of the spell must still be active."

That was a lot to think about. Adalyn was soon distracted, however, as Venlian stood. "Come. We mustn't be late for the war council."

"What? War council?"

"Yes. You asked if I was meeting with the royals, and I am, as well as their advisors. Much has been discussed in the time we were away, and the return of the keystones has prompted a call to action."

Adalyn felt a little lightheaded at this news. Meeting with royalty was nerve-wracking in its own right, and now a whole roomful of important people would be present, as well. She longed more than ever for her simple life in the kitchens.

Venlian didn't seem to share her anxiety, as he led her to the designated place with an easy gait. A large stone table with more than a dozen high-backed chairs around it sat in the center of the room. Alternating chairs and benches along the walls, which had no decoration hanging on them, made the room feel unwelcoming and mysterious in use. Following Venlian inside, she chose a spot near him on a bench, trying to stay out of the way of the people mulling around before things started.

King Thanmog strode into the room, taking the largest seat at the head of the table, followed by King Coeus and Queen Tillie, who sat on either side of him. All conversation hushed as everyone else found their seats.

"Thank you, everyone, for taking this time to meet. With the keystones back, we will be able to awaken our golems later today and prepare to take back the capital above. Has everyone had a chance to read the debriefing from Venlian of his expedition to Chors?" King Thanmog's deep rasp echoed in the room.

A collection of nods and mumbled acknowledgments followed the king's question.

"Good. Today, we will finalize our plan of attack. King

Coeus, Queen Tillie, do you have any additional information to add before we begin?"

Adalyn thought King Coeus looked more relaxed than he'd been after their escape from the castle. She wondered just what had changed to make him so comfortable with this group.

"I do not," he responded, leaning back in his chair, holding a mug of ale in one hand and fiddling with a coin in the other. He looked over to Queen Tillie.

"I also have no new information to add before we begin. I do have a question, though." Queen Tillie turned and looked directly at Adalyn. "Who is our visitor? Perhaps we should address that before revealing our plans."

The room seemed to shrink in size as every pair of eyes turned toward her.

"Ah, of course. You two, I doubt, have had much interaction. This is Adalyn. She is a… servant of mine." King Coeus took a moment, as though deciding exactly how to explain Adalyn. "She was instrumental in leading us here and facilitating the expedition to Chors. What can we do for you, Adalyn?"

Not sure how to address the people present, or even *whom* to address, Adalyn stood. "I'm sorry to interrupt. I have some information that may be of use."

Queen Tillie leaned forward, resting her chin in her hand. "I remember you now. You helped us get out of the castle during the attack."

"Yes, Your Majesty."

"Hmm… go on."

"I have just returned from scouting the capital and

castle to get a feel of what is going on. It's much worse than I imagined."

King Thanmog raised his bushy eyebrows. "You scouted? How did you get into the city? You're sure you weren't seen?"

"My worldwalking skills helped me go unnoticed."

"I imagine those skills are similar to those that allowed you to escape my cells?"

"Yes, sir." Adalyn couldn't look him in the face, she was so nervous.

King Coeus smirked, and Adalyn glanced at Venlian, who gave her an encouraging look. She took a deep breath and continued, detailing her discussion with Glenda and their scouting trip.

"Large numbers have moved into the city, and more are due to arrive soon. The dungeon is filled with nobles and those who worked in the castle. Official buildings have become prisons for the citizens who are not being put to work building defenses around the city. They are preparing for us to attack."

Queen Tillie looked concerned. "You say that large numbers of soldiers are in the city. Do you know how many?"

"I can't be entirely sure, but Glenda estimated at least twenty thousand are in the city and the surrounding country."

King Thanmog let out a huff. "It's worse than our own scouts have been able to tell us. We will have to plan intelligently. What kind of defenses are they putting up? Tell us everything you can remember."

For the next hour, Adalyn shared every detail she

could recall. Afterward, the group decided to take a short break before reconvening to decide a plan of action, which thankfully didn't require her attendance. Holding back to allow the room to empty before she left, she noticed a presence next to her.

"Queen Tillie, how may I be of service to you?"

"I want to thank you. If it wasn't for your quick thinking when we needed to escape, I doubt we would be alive now. Even with the distress of my daughter's condition, you kept your cool and were patient."

"May I ask, how is Queen May?"

"Doing very well, thank you. She had a beautiful little boy while you were gone. When you get the chance, you should visit. I'm sure she would appreciate thanking you in person."

That explained King Coeus' relaxed manner. What sovereign wouldn't be more at ease when an heir had been born? Nodding, Adalyn smiled. "I will do that. Thank you."

"Do you know what you will do once this is over? Will you work in the kitchen again?"

"I honestly don't know what I will do after all of this. I really love working in the kitchen, but I've had a lot happen that has changed things for me."

"You seem to be a good person, an honest person. I'm always looking for trustworthy people to add to my personal caravan. Being in a nomadic court isn't so bad, and I'm sure we could find a room for you in our winter quarters. Just something to think on." Without giving Adalyn a chance to respond, Queen Tillie smiled and then walked out of the room.

She began to follow suit when a firm voice stopped her. "You didn't tell me you went scouting."

Adalyn was surprised at the glower on Venlian's face. She didn't think elves could be angry. She had always thought of them as higher beings who had mastered their emotions.

"What's wrong with that?" she asked.

"I always thought Glenda had more common sense than to put you in danger," Venlian said, his eyes flashing. "I… we need you. They all need you. Your ability can change the outcome of this reignited war."

Adalyn huffed. "Seriously? Did you see that in my book?" she fired back. "Look, I went in my spirit form. I wasn't in any danger. No one could see or harm me."

Venlian rubbed the bridge of his nose with his thumb and index finger, eyes closed. "*Most* wouldn't be able to see you. There may be some who could still sense you and do something about it. Just… next time, let me know. Take me with you."

"I don't know how to take another person with me yet," she replied, crossing her arms. "I'm still not entirely sure how we all got through the gateway together."

He sighed and looked up at her. "Take the remainder of the day to rest. I have meetings all day. Later, I will work with you and help you so that you can take me along next time. I'm sure Glenda is helping you how she can, she always was good at that, but her ability didn't extend to bringing others on her travels. Do you promise not to do anything foolish?"

Incensed by the implication, but not wanting this conversation to go on any longer, she relented. "Fine. I can't wait forever to figure this out, though. I'm sure the king will want me to check things out at least once more before we attack."

"Agreed."

With that, Adalyn turned her back on him and left the room, deciding to look for Eridu. Maybe she would have something less stressful to distract her with.

FIFTEEN

After over an hour of wandering and multiple cases of misdirection by well-meaning people, Adalyn finally found Eridu in the largest cave she'd ever seen (besides the massive cavern that housed the old dwarven city, that is). It was some distance from both the old and new cities, and at first, she thought it was odd that the room was full of rock mounds of varying sizes. Then it dawned on her that these had to be the golems they'd been referring to. The cave was full of them, several hundred at least.

Working her way through the room, Adalyn was careful not to touch any of the golems or bother any of the many dwarves at work. She noticed that each of the golems were unique—a variety of colors and textures, with runes etched into them. Some were an amalgam of multiple types of stones. It was clear that they were each as different as the dwarves whose spirits had been preserved in them.

A waving hand among the mounds caught her interest, and relief filled her at the sight of her friend.

"I was hoping you would show up soon!" Eridu's excitement was clearly evident by her wide grin. Pulling a long, metal tool out of her hair, she bent and removed a spot on the golem piled in front of her.

"I see you haven't woken them up yet."

"No, not yet. We have to make sure we do this right and find the highest-ranking of the golems to wake first. Try to avoid some of the chaos."

"Is this the one you're planning to wake first?"

"He is. Look at this rune here." Adalyn leaned closer to look where Eridu pointed, at a half-circle with a four-pointed star set in the center, etched into an especially vibrant dark blue stone in the pile of varying grays and blues. "This is the mark of a general. We haven't found any other golems with this high of a ranking."

"A general! I had no idea they would have their own military."

"I wouldn't necessarily call it that. From what I've read, they were organized into military units, but most of the ranking was to keep order long-term, since the golems can live indefinitely."

"What did dwarves do with them when they weren't needed?"

"That's the genius of them. Once the keystones are removed, they become dormant. Remember the keystones we grabbed? I took two different types. If one is inserted into the golem, they respond to every command given to them and can even mimic the movements of whoever has control over them. The other allows them free will. Remember, these aren't just stone soldiers. These are our ancestors who did incredible things. They contributed to our society in such a way that we didn't want to lose them."

"Which one are you planning on using?"

"That's been a pretty serious discussion among our royal dignitaries. It's come down to waking up only a few with their own will intact. Once we've spoken with them, we can consider the best method for waking the others."

"Sounds like we are in for an interesting afternoon."

"That we are, and it looks like our keystone is here," Eridu said as a dwarf brought her something. "Stand behind me and try not to get in the way, just in case our friend here doesn't wake up in a good mood."

Adalyn moved out of the way and anxiously watched as Eridu's team inserted a black cylinder into a slot below the rune denoting the golem's rank. The keystone seemed tiny, compared to the golem. Adalyn wondered at such a small thing having the power to bring such a large creature to life. The ground rumbled as the rocks shifted and separated into limbs, a torso, and finally, a head.

A loud groan sounded from the golem as it straightened to stand. Adalyn's head craned back as she gazed up at it while it did so, marveling when it reached a height over three times her own. "Thank you for that, my young ones," a deep voice rumbled.

Eridu's fingers tapped excitedly on her arms as she fiddled with a small, thin metal pick in her mouth. "It's no trouble at all. I'm Eridu. It's a pleasure to finally meet you."

"I know who you are."

Eridu's fiddling stopped. "Excuse me? You do?"

"Golems do not sleep. I've been watching and listening since my keystone was stolen from me."

"Oh…" Eridu looked at a loss for words, as did everyone else in the cave. All of the dwarves had stopped their work to watch the golem awaken.

"No need to fret. You've been nothing but kind to us, and now you have allowed me freedom—something that I haven't had in a very long time. You may call me Iolite."

"It's wonderful to meet you, Iolite. I assume that means I don't need to inform you of everything that's going on, since we've been discussing it while at our work. Do you understand how and why we woke you?"

"I do."

"Are you willing to help us?"

The golem eyed the group in contemplation. "I do not like going to battle. None of my troops do. It's why we have lasted so long while many of our friends are gone. If we are given the opportunity to do this without being controlled and can decide our own future after, then I think we can come to an agreement."

Eridu put her hands in her pockets. "I don't have full rights to offer you everything you've asked for. It may take some time to get someone who can offer all of that down here. I'm willing to wait if you are. What I can commit to is that I personally will not put in a keystone that would take away your free will, neither will anyone on my team. We will stand up for you and your rights as dwarven citizens. However, if you choose to harm our people, we will be forced to act."

"I understand. From what I have heard before you activated me, I believe you will stick to your promises. I agree to help you, and when it's convenient for me to speak on behalf of my troops to your king, I would like to request to have the rest of the golems activated. It's been so very long since we were able to move."

"It sounds like we have a deal."

Eridu and Iolite discussed which of the golems to awaken next, as she'd been authorized to wake a few, then began giving directions to her team as they worked on activating those golems.

Adalyn stood back and watched as the golems around her began moving, hoping none of them were going to step on her. If only she had considered moving to the outside of the cave instead of remaining inside. At this point, it was more dangerous to move than to stay put.

"Aye! Those filthy humans! Five hundred years of lying in a heap after years of putting up with their cockiness and commands. I'm not going to help the lot of them! I refuse!" A stocky golem of red, orange, and yellow swirled stones angrily spat out at his commander.

"You will behave, Carnelian, or I will remove that keystone myself." Iolite stared down the other golem.

"I think you may have forgotten how briefly humans live. I'm sure they've evolved in more ways than one. These are not the same people who put us here." The soft, older woman's voice surprised Adalyn as she realized it came from a slightly more slender, bright blue golem with gold flecks and veins running through her. The golem turned toward Adalyn. "This one doesn't seem so bad."

She froze. A golem was talking to her, and her body wouldn't move.

"Well, now you've scared her, Lazuli," a young man's voice emanated from the pearlescent white golem to her left. "Don't worry, we aren't all that bad. Some of us are just waking up a bit grumpy. Being stuck in one spot for so long can have odd effects on anyone."

Forcing her lips to move, Adalyn responded, "Sorry. I don't know what to say. I'm Adalyn. Really, we aren't all bad. I can't vouch for everyone you will deal with, though."

The white golem chuckled.

"Don't worry, dear. We are no threat to you at the moment. Carnelian always was a bit of a hothead, but he means no harm. He's a big softie deep down," Lazuli said while inspecting herself.

"Yeah—deep, deep down," the white golem added. "I'm Merit. It's a pleasure to meet you." He then turned toward his leader. "Do you think maybe I should handle the negotiations with the king? I am a royal and know how to work with them."

A small pebble hit Merit on the head. "*Were* royal, you cocky nitwit. When you became a golem, you gave that up. Don't go putting on airs and acting like you're above us. We especially don't want the humans to think you're something you're not," Carnelian spouted while glaring at Merit.

Iolite held up his hand. "Stop your bickering. Merit, I would appreciate your experience in the negotiations. You will join me when we meet with the kings. Adalyn, it's nice to meet you. We golems should really have time to discuss things together, if only to ensure that everyone is behaving properly."

"Of course. I wouldn't want to intrude, but I would like to come back sometime. I've got some things I would like to ask you about, if you wouldn't mind. I want to understand what happened here," Adalyn said.

Eridu nodded exuberantly. "I'd like to know, as well, and take it down for our history. In the meantime, I need to report to my superiors."

"I can see the benefit of that. Until later, then."

Adalyn watched as the golems gathered together, already beginning an animated discussion. Her life seemed to be getting stranger and stranger, and she realized she didn't entirely dislike that fact.

She left the golems' cavern, not knowing what exactly to do now. Everyone she knew was busy, and she really didn't feel she had a purpose. Deciding to wander in the old city, she explored the dilapidated buildings.

She investigated an old bathhouse with white and navy blue tiles lining the communal bath. Most of the buildings were empty, and many were filled with rubble from caved-in walls and ceilings. It was difficult to tell if the damage was from the battle or from time. Stone walkways arched overhead, connecting the dwellings built into the rocks above, though some of those had toppled, as well.

An open intersection, with a toppled statue of the most fearsome dwarf she had ever seen, appeared ahead of her. This crossroad, wider than any other she had come across, appeared to be one of the highest-trafficked areas.

Curious what the dwarves would consider so important to put at this kind of intersection, she ventured into the safest-looking of the buildings. Most of the building was empty like the rest she had investigated, containing a few crumbling wood pieces, the occasional cup, and odd stone stacks.

Working her way through a section of collapsed wall, a metal door with a padlock on it drew her attention. She pulled on the door, hoping it would open, but it didn't budge. She had to give the dwarves credit—they knew how to do decent metalwork.

Deciding she wouldn't get in that way, Adalyn touched the door with her hand, allowing herself to sink into it. Feeling her spirit's hand go through the door without the rest of her, she decided to attempt poking her head through to take a peek. She rested her forehead on the door and placed both hands up next to it, then eased her way through.

The space was pitch black. While her body's eyes wouldn't have been able to see a thing, she was pleasantly surprised to find her spirit had no issue making out the shapes of weapons on rows of stands throughout the room. Shelves lining one wall were filled with parchment rolls, and racks hanging on the walls held a variety of weapons she didn't recognize.

Pulling her head back to her body, she attempted the door again, only to find it still unmovable. Excited by her new discovery, she hurried back and found Venlian leaving a meeting. After convincing him to check out what she'd found, Adalyn hurried Venlian back to the mysterious room.

"Can you open it?"

Two thin, metal tools protruded from the lock, and one remained in his mouth, forcing Venlian to mumble something unintelligible.

"What?" Adalyn asked.

He paused to take the tool out of his mouth. "I said, if you will allow me a moment, I think I might."

She paced back and forth behind him, pausing every few repetitions to watch his progress. Finally, a soft click sounded from the door as he removed the lock. Slowly opening the door, he held a lantern up, a small smile turning up one corner of his mouth. "Well, you've found something quite useful here."

Following him into the room, she gently touched a large battle-axe with a stark white handle and refrained from squealing. "I did?"

"Yes, you did. We've been discussing the short supply of weapons for the upcoming battle. We don't have enough time to make one for everyone. These can be cleaned up and used."

"Aren't I lucky? I'm glad I can help."

"You truly don't understand how lucky you are. These aren't just any weapons. These are enchanted, like the sword I gave you. They can kill death slaughs and any other cursed beast the enemy brings with them. None had been found in storage. It was a top concern. That gives me an idea." He turned to her with raised eyebrows, still wearing that smug half-smile. "Up for some practice using your ability and taking an individual with you?"

"Yeah! What do you have in mind?"

"Let's go back to my library. I think I have another way to help us win this battle."

"What if I can't do it with you?"

"You can. You just have to try."

"Sound advice. Just try. Anything extra to assist the trying? I don't want to accidentally drop you in whatever I travel through to get there. Heck, I don't even know if I travel through something at all. I just appear there. What if only part of you arrives, while half of your body is left here, or—"

"Slow down. You're getting yourself worked up. Taking me along should be fairly simple, and if it doesn't go as you plan, I have my own abilities to fall back on. Now, imagine me as another object you are taking with you. Do you have to think about taking the clothes you're wearing?"

"No."

"Why not?"

"It's just a part of me."

Venlian looked at her expectantly, waiting.

Adalyn raised a brow. "I don't know exactly what you're trying to say, but I'm not getting it."

"Think of me as an extension of you. Grab hold of me and try taking me with you."

"Can we try with something simpler first? I'm still not sure about taking a living thing with me."

"All right." Venlian went outside the building and came back with a mouse. Adalyn wondered how he'd managed to find the small creature, and so quickly at that. "Take this little fellow with you from here to the building across the street."

She didn't move. "What if it bites me?"

"It's not going to bite you. Don't do anything to startle it, and it won't have any reason to protect itself."

"Oh, sure, being transported suddenly from one place to the next certainly wouldn't startle anything."

Venlian gave her a look. "You can do this. Just take it and try."

Transferring the mouse from his hands took a few minutes. Several starts and squeals emitted from Adalyn before she finally held the little mouse in her hands. She tried to reappear with the mouse across the street, but nothing happened.

"Maybe I can't do it. You and Glenda have both told me that abilities vary from person to person."

"You can do this. Really think about the mouse. Feel the texture of its fur. Become aware of its presence in your hands, not as a separate thing, but as another part of your hand."

Trying again, she blinked and found herself in the other building.

"I did it!" Her sudden movement in her excitement caused the mouse to drop to the ground and escape.

Venlian walked in. "Well done. See, you can transport a living thing without incident. Are you ready to try it with me?"

"Fine, but if you end up spliced in half or show up naked, just remember that I warned you and it's not my fault."

"Agreed."

Putting her hand on Venlian's shoulder, Adalyn closed her eyes and tried to take in every detail of him she could while thinking of his library. His scent of lemon, thyme, and old parchment. The feel of his woven jacket in her hand. She opened her eyes for a moment and noticed the dark glow around him she'd seen when they first met. She assumed it had to be his aura. Looking down at herself, she realized she could see her own as well. An idea popped into her head. Taking in his details, she attempted to connect her aura to his and closed her eyes again, picturing the library. She opened her eyes again, and then jumped gleefully.

"I did it!"

Venlian nodded. "Obviously."

She scoffed at his attitude. "Your exuberance is overwhelming."

"I need to go speak with a few people. Do you mind if I leave you here in the library? I can send someone with food."

"Not at all," she said, though her heart skipped a beat at the thought of meeting more elves. "Would you mind pulling a few books for me, though?"

"What would you like?"

"I want to see the people who've had the same ability as me; see how they used it, and possibly learn a bit about how to make it work."

"That's a very wise idea. I will fetch those before I leave. Give me a few minutes."

As Venlian began pulling books from the shelves, Adalyn wandered over to a set of overstuffed chairs with a small table in front of a tall, stained-glass window.

Soon, Venlian came back with a pile of books. "These

should be safe for you to read. Just be careful with them because there are no other copies."

Adalyn fingered the pages of the first book with adoration. "Thank you so much!"

Once settled and left to her own devices, Adalyn opened the book, which had a dark blue binding with *Mark Edgwyn Inglewood* inscribed in copper on the cover. The words in the book stayed in place, unlike the book she had previously seen here. As she began to read, the words in the book called to her. A familiar pull on her spirit encouraged her to place her hand on the center of the book. As she did so, the words shifted into an image, and her spirit was pulled into the book.

A room much like the one she had claimed in the Banneret dormitory surrounded her. An older man with short, salt-and-pepper hair and a neatly trimmed beard sat in a chair facing the door, sharpening a longsword.

A knock made the man look up. "Come in."

A teenaged boy poked his head in. "Captain, they are ready for you."

"I'll be there in just a moment, Edward." The man stood and stretched his back. He took a moment to admire his handiwork, then sheathed his sword and mumbled to himself, "Another pointless meeting with a group of hotheads. Who needs a war council when there's no war?"

The rest of the book appeared in a series of short scenes, with Adalyn standing by as a witness to the man's life. She was able to see him make use of his worldwalking ability and wondered at the ease in which he used it. Would she feel that confident someday?

After watching his peaceful death with his family at home, Adalyn's spirit returned to her body in the library. She put the book down and picked up the next one. This one was a darker shade of blue, with *Skylar Bluebell* printed on the cover in ornate curls.

Her ability called her into the book as before. She found herself in a pub filled with a boisterous crowd. Her attention was drawn to a group in a corner wearing matching blue fitted jackets and leather breeches.

A clearly inebriated man spilled his drink on one of the group while passing by.

The victim stood, shaking the front of her jacket in an attempt to flick the drink off. "Excuse you!"

"What?" The inebriated man wavered in his spot, holding his ground.

"I said, excuse you. Are you going to apologize for spilling your drink on me?"

"Nah," he drawled. "It's not my fault. You were in the way."

The Banneret leaned in, and Adalyn noticed the glint of steel between the two individuals. "I was in your way while sitting in my chair, minding my own business? Are you sure?"

A slight hunch formed in the man's back, a clear indication that he had a knife pointed at his stomach, poised to empty its contents.

"So sorry," he rushed. "My mistake, ma'am."

A small yelp from the man got the attention of several other Banneret at the table, and they jumped up and pulled the woman off the man.

"What did you call me?!" she shrieked.

"I'm sure he didn't mean any disrespect by calling you ma'am. Some people find it a compliment," the Banneret holding on to her knife arm said soothingly, trying to calm her.

"Ma'am is for old ladies! Do I look old?"

A bearded man still in his seat chuckled. "If you would ever make yourself look like the proper lady you are, Skylar, maybe people wouldn't think you looked so old."

Skylar turned on her heel, nearly knocking those restraining her over as she did so. The inebriated man escaped while her attention was diverted. "Some of us have other things to worry about besides how beautiful we look, Garret," she sneered, spit shooting from her mouth as she pushed out his name.

"Oh, dear girl, if only you knew the power that a little bit of charm really has."

Skylar shook herself loose from the group's hands and sat down in a huff. She sheathed her knife and downed what was left of her mug of ale before waving to the barmaid for another.

Adalyn stared at the hilt of the knife, noticing similarities between it, Mark Edgwyn Inglewood's sword hilt, and her own. A thought began to form in her mind as she jumped from moment to moment in Skylar's rough-and-tumble life. The woman had used her worldwalking during many a brawl, disappearing from one place to surprise her opponent from somewhere else.

Hours passed as she previewed several more people's lives until she picked up Glenda's book. She almost put it back down, but decided to glance in it anyway. The first chunk looked similar to the other books she had been reading.

Noticing a mention of Glenda's sword as she flipped through, Adalyn chose to let herself be pulled into the moment, and a forge soon surrounded her.

"Are you ready to do this?" a bulky, red, lizard-like man with rows of sharp horns on his head and wearing a thick leather apron asked a very youthful Glenda.

"What if I mess it up?"

"Listen with your ability, and you won't mess it up. Overthink it, and this will be much more difficult."

Glenda tentatively raised her sword and placed it in the roaring fire. Adalyn watched as it was reworked into a new shape and size almost as if it was forging itself. Glenda seemed to enter a sort of trance as she worked the steel. When she was finished, Adalyn recognized the new shape as the same as her own.

The man put his hand gently on Glenda's shoulder as she swayed a bit, still not quite herself. "Well done. Leave it here, then come back and finish up after you get some rest."

"It spoke to me," Glenda murmured, eyes glazed.

"They tend to do that. Every Banneret's connection with their item is a bit different, but if you are in tune with your ability when you claim your item, it truly guides you to transform it into something that will amplify your magic. The more in tune you are when you do this, the stronger that connection and amplification will be."

Glenda just nodded, turned, and slowly walked away, waving a belated thanks behind her.

Pulling out of the scene, Adalyn reached for her sword

and looked it over with fresh eyes. She hadn't realized it was Glenda's sword. Why hadn't she said anything?

It was difficult to process everything she had just seen, but she was invigorated and overwhelmed at the prospect of all she'd learned. When they returned, Glenda needed to be at the top of her list of people to talk to. Adalyn had so many questions.

Venlian came back to the library to find Adalyn asleep on the chair he had left her in, mumbling nonsense. After climbing over the scattered books around her, he squatted in front of the chair and said her name. She didn't stir. After several more attempts, he decided to try gently shaking her arm to wake her.

Her eyes slowly opened and focused on him. "I fell asleep."

"It appears so."

Slowly sitting up, she wiped a bit of drool from her mouth and noticed a wet spot where her head had been. "I am so sorry. I didn't mean to."

A small smile formed on his lips. "Of course you didn't. You aren't the first to fall asleep in here, and I'm sure you won't be the last."

"Your meeting, how did it go?"

Venlian stood back up and stretched. "Rather well, actually. They've agreed to assist us by sending weapons, as well as an army of volunteers."

"Really? That's wonderful! Much better than I could have ever expected."

"There's a catch, though. You have to transport them there."

"I can't do that!"

"Of course you can. You won't be expected to do it today. They have to gather the weapons and put out the call for volunteers. We will start small and use this as a training exercise for your ability."

"Why can't you do it?"

"I am limited, only able to take myself from place to place. If you recall, I had to lead you back to my library."

"I see," Adalyn said, mulling it over. "We had better start out very slow, though. Just transporting myself wears me out over time. I can only imagine how exhausting it will be doing multiple people and items."

"You can do it. I've seen amazing strength in you. Tomorrow, we will start. Let's head back and get some rest." Venlian bent to pick up the books around her. "Did you find what you were looking for in the books?"

Adalyn joined him in stacking them back up and depositing them on a table. "Actually, I did." She'd seen many worldwalkers use their abilities, and was excited to experiment with her own—after they'd retaken the castle, that is.

When they got back, however, all Adalyn could think about was just how exhausted she was. Normally, reading would be relaxing, but using her ability to see inside each book had drained her entirely. Leaving Venlian to update the leaders, she headed back through the ruins toward her quarters. Barely acknowledging the spirits in the common room, she stumbled into bed, expecting to fall asleep instantly.

Unfortunately, she soon realized that wouldn't be the case.

Her mind wouldn't shut up about everything that she had seen. Looping around each individual's life, transporting the elves, the reforging of her weapon, she began to get anxious. Images of Isabella lying in her cell flashed through her head. Her chest tightened until it was difficult to breathe, and no matter what she did, she couldn't get it to stop. Feeling like she was either going to faint or throw up, she decided to try and find some water.

Slowly working her way back to the Banneret common room, stopping several times to lean on a wall and take deep breaths, she finally entered the room and sat on a couch, putting her head in her hands.

"Are you all right?" Glenda asked.

"I'm not sure. I need… something."

"Several of the king's soldiers brought provisions in here earlier. You should grab some food and water."

"Why would they do that? Everything is provided for them by the dwarves for now."

"I have a feeling that King Coeus is just preparing in case things go south. It's difficult to reverse generations of distrust. It will take years of patience and everyone treating each other as equals before things begin to change. Go and get something to drink, at least."

Adalyn grabbed dried meat and vegetables and a cup of mulled cider and sat back down. That first sip felt like heaven, and after a few bites of food, she started to feel the tightness in her chest easing.

"You sure you're all right?"

"Yeah, just not feeling myself. A lot has happened, and I just have a great deal of weight on my shoulders. It feels as though much of how things turn out is starting to rely on me."

Glenda smiled. "Oh, my dear, sweet, young one. That's how it goes when you develop an ability. The Banneret were not originally formed for the king's purposes. It was so people who were blessed with these abilities had a community to support them. They only started working for the king years later when there was a need. They were paid well for their services, and over time, housing was established for those who wanted it, and everything became central here."

"Can I ask you a question? About the Banneret?"

"Ask away."

Not sure how much she could say without Glenda feeling like she had overstepped, Adalyn hesitated. "I just got back from Venlian's library, and I asked him if I could see the books of those who have had this same ability. I saw several of their lives."

"How exactly did you see their lives?"

"I would touch the book and feel my ability tell me that I could enter. I was shown scenes from the person's life, as if I were an observer in the room." Seeing Glenda's intrigued look, she stammered, "Is that not normal?"

"I've heard of the library that the elves have, but I don't know of any human who has been there. What you did is certainly a new twist to our ability."

"Oh."

"No, dear, an exciting and intriguing one. You were asking about something you saw?"

"Well, I noticed everyone had an object with the same symbols on them as my sword. I saw someone forge theirs." She wasn't ready to talk about the fact that she had Glenda's sword. She had so much to process already.

"Yes, it's a tradition, and part of the ability itself. The items sort of attune themselves to the current ability holder, and how that person manifests the ability will change the item."

"What about the forge? Should I go to it? It was mentioned that it would help amplify my ability."

Glenda laughed, and Adalyn heard chuckles from the other spirits in the room that she wasn't paying attention to. "You don't just go to it. In fact, none of us could even tell you where it is."

"I don't understand. If the Banneret go there to do this, how do you not know where it is?"

"The forge master is a being all his own, and his forge is a magical place. There's actually several. All hidden with communities that support and protect them. You don't find it, it finds you. Does that make sense?"

"Not in the slightest."

"I promise, when the time is right, the forge will find you and you will know what to do."

"If the item is sort of attached to the person with the ability, where are the other items when they aren't claimed? Where would they be now, or where have they been all these years? I'm assuming that all Banneret have them?"

"They're somewhere out there. They aren't easily destroyed and tend to find their way to their owners when they are needed. I imagine that Banneret who were on the other side supporting our army when the living spell froze them in time still hold their own."

The idea had never crossed her mind that there would be others with abilities still in Chors, but it made sense. Adalyn would have to tell Venlian about the living spell's effect on time. It explained the difference they'd experienced while on the expedition.

Having calmed down and able to breathe better, a wave of exhaustion hit her. "I think I'm ready to get some sleep now. Can we finish this chat later? I've got more questions."

"Of course. One thing, though: I think we need to do another scouting mission soon. Things seem to be ramping up in the city, and you should see so you can report."

Adalyn nodded as she left the room, the call of her pillow becoming more demanding with each step.

SEVENTEEN

The trips back and forth bringing the elvish support over the next week took a lot out of Adalyn, but with Venlian's support, she was able to do it. She wasn't necessarily tired enough to sleep between, but the need for rest and food to recharge was ever-present. She could feel herself getting a better grasp of her ability with each trip and had even started taking more than one person with her at a time, but after her fifth trip today, she needed to eat.

Leaving the building she'd been transporting the elves to, she set off in search of food. Turning a corner, a familiar voice hollered out, "Isn't that the squishy human who was there when they woke us?"

A smile spread on her face when she heard a swift *thunk* accompanied by, "Hey, stupid, they're all squishy compared to us. You were once squishy, too, remember?"

Turning toward the group, she found the four golems filling up an entire dwarven street.

"Hello," she greeted simply. How was one supposed to address a group of rocky giants, anyway?

"It's good to see you again," Iolite responded.

"You, too. I hadn't expected to see you here."

Light caught just above Merit's eye, in what she assumed was him raising a stony eyebrow. "Why exactly wouldn't we be here?"

"I just… I don't know. I guess I didn't think about where you would be after you got your keystones. What have you been up to?"

Carnelian harrumphed. "Lots of boring meetings talking about the old war and fixing up old buildings."

"Why are you fixing up the old buildings?"

Lazuli's soft voice floated over to her. "Someone's been helping the elves get here." She looked at Adalyn with a twinkle in her eye. "Between us golems waking and the influx of humans and elves, the dwarves are running out of room to put everyone. We will soon move to the old dwarven city as repairs get further along."

All of the golems nodded as they looked at Adalyn. She tried not to squirm under their watchful gaze.

"Been up to anything other than transporting elves?" Merit asked.

"That's taken a lot of my time, but I have been spending what's left in the old Banneret area between here and the castle."

Iolite leaned forward intently. "What do you know of the Banneret?"

Not sure if his reaction was good or bad, she almost whispered, "I am one."

He grumbled a chuckle. "I wondered how you were getting the elves here and why only you could do it. It all makes sense now. You're a worldwalker, aren't you?"

"I am. How did you know?"

"I've known a few. Tend to be good people, but every once in a while, they go a bit crazy with power. I've seen the ability abandon a few when they got too far gone."

The idea that could happen hadn't even occurred to her. She didn't know what to say.

Sensing her unease, Lazuli spoke up. "Any plans for the next while?"

"Today, just transporting elves. They have something going on tomorrow afternoon, so I was thinking about doing some scouting in the…" the grins that all of the golems suddenly sported made her hesitate, "…city. Why are you looking at me like that?"

Carnelian smirked. "Want some company?"

"I'm sure your information would be considered more reliable with a few extra sets of eyes," Iolite added.

"Shouldn't you stay hidden, so they don't know you exist?"

Merit scoffed. "Are you planning on getting caught?"

"Well, no…"

Lazuli put her hand on Adalyn's arm. "We want to go with you. We have ways of keeping ourselves hidden, and in all seriousness, I really need a change of scenery. Even if it's just for a few minutes."

The group nodded at her in agreement.

"Fine, do you know how to get to the Banneret common room?"

More nodding.

"Meet me there tomorrow after lunch. Don't be late, or I'm going without you." She had a feeling this was a very bad idea. She said her goodbyes and continued on to find something to eat.

After finishing her meal, she decided to wander around the old city as she made her way back to see what repairs had been done. The area along her walk to the Banneret common room hadn't been changed, but as she investigated the buildings skirting a newly opened entrance to the new dwarven city, there was fresh grout and stone patching broken walls. A few lights shone through windows, and teams carrying armloads of supplies made Adalyn smile. She could almost see what this city would have looked like when it was thriving.

She spotted Nolan among one of the groups repairing walls, fitting large carved stones into place. She couldn't help but notice the way his linen shirt stuck to his muscles as he lifted a stone block onto a short wall.

"Need a hand?" she asked as she approached.

Nolan jerked, dropping the stone suddenly at the sound of her voice. "I figured you wouldn't be up for this sort of heavy lifting. Besides, I heard they were keeping you busy filling these homes with elves," Nolan responded, stretching his back.

"I do my best, but we've still got a lot of people to get here. It keeps me busy."

Wiping the sweat from his brow, his face lit up with a smile. "I've missed you. What brings you down here?"

Her face heated at the realization that she had missed him as well. "I heard about the repairs and thought I would check them out while stretching my legs."

"What do you think?"

She cast her gaze around the area. "It feels like this place is coming back to life. I know most of the elves will go back home after things settle down, but it's really exciting to see everyone working together."

"I understand what you're saying. Just a few months ago, I would have called anyone a liar if they'd told me I would be fixing up dwarven housing for elves to live in."

Nodding, Adalyn leaned against the side of a building. "You're not wrong. I would have, too. Just a thought—are these houses tall enough for the elves? I mean, the dwarves are short, and these doorways seem kind of small."

Nolan chuckled. "Some of the elves have had a few bumps. At least the dwarves seem to like high ceilings, so that's not an issue. For now, the guests will have to deal with the short doorways." He nudged her arm and their gazes met, "What are you up to later?"

"I've got more transporting runs to make today, and I'll probably crash after. I'm getting better at my ability, but it's still exhausting."

"What about tomorrow? I heard no runs were happening tomorrow afternoon."

Adalyn paused for a moment, trying to decide how much she should tell him. "Just how did you know that?"

"Since we got down here, I feel like we haven't really seen each other. So, I might have asked around to see when you may be free."

Her heart warmed at his admission. "I've missed you, too. But I'm going out for a bit."

His brow lifted. "Out where?"

She pointed her finger up.

"You're kidding me, right?"

She shook her head.

"Why are you chancing going into the city?"

"Glenda wants to show me something up there. I'm just going to stay hidden and gather some information. Several of the golems and…"

Concern written on his face, Nolan turned toward her. "No one other than our scouts should be going into the capital. It could ruin our element of surprise for the attack la… Wait, golems are going with you?"

She shrugged. "A couple. It's really hard to say no to a golem."

"Understandable," he said after contemplating that for a moment. "I'm coming, too."

From the tension in his body, she couldn't tell if he was mad or concerned. "Excuse me? Why are you coming?"

"I have nothing against the golems, but I'm not the kind of person who trusts others blindly. Do you have anyone else coming with you? Anyone you can fully trust to have your back?"

Knowing Glenda couldn't actually do anything to defend her, Adalyn responded, "Not really."

He crossed his arms and gave her a determined look. Adalyn knew she wouldn't get away with going without him.

"Fine, you can come. After lunch, meet me in the Banneret common room." She pointed a finger at him, nearly touching his nose, "Do not tell anyone else, and don't be late. I'm already taking too large of a group as it is."

Turning away from the goofy grin of victory on his face and the knot it made in her stomach, she had a feeling this was a very bad idea indeed.

EIGHTEEN

Stepping into the common room the next day, Adalyn saw Nolan awkwardly standing near the fireplace watching the four rather large stone golems. Each stood in various poses of the least relaxing-looking attempts of comfort she had ever seen, which made her smile and took a bit of the edge off of her nerves. That immediately changed when all five pairs of eyes turned in her direction.

Clasping her hands in front of her and rocking on the balls of her feet, Adalyn spoke to the group. "Who's ready to go do something quite possibly very stupid?"

The tension in the room eased as everyone chuckled.

"When am I not ready to do something stupid?" Carnelian asked with a mischievous grin.

"I'm going ahead for a moment to scout our landing spot and make sure it's clear," Adalyn said.

After everyone nodded, Adalyn sat in a chair, let her spirit leave her body, and made her way to the capital. Once she found a safe, quiet space to transport everyone to, she quickly returned in spirit form, only to find the group frantically fussing over her body while Glenda stood to the side, laughing.

"Maybe next time tell them what you're doing. They all think you just sat down and died."

"Are you serious? It's not like it's the first time Nolan has seen me do this!"

"Are you sure?"

Adalyn tried to remember and realized that he actually hadn't.

"You're the one who decided you needed company for this trip. I suggested that you go in your spirit form so you didn't get caught."

"Yeah, I got caught up when they brought up that having information from more than one person would be more reliable. This is a terrible idea…"

"I could have told you that."

"Technically, you did."

Rolling her eyes and exhaling a deep breath of nothing, Adalyn returned to her body and brushed the many hands off of her. "I'm fine! Stop touching me."

The golems backed off, but Nolan stayed, trapping her in the chair. "What do you mean, you're fine? You were just dead!"

"I promise you, I was quite alive. Part of my ability allows me to leave my physical body behind and walk with just my spirit. I thought that was safer than showing up suddenly. As a spirit, I can check stuff out without anyone seeing me."

Glenda's voice whispered next to her ear, "Almost anyone."

"Hush, you."

Nolan raised an eyebrow. "No one said anything. Are you sure you're all right?"

"Quite sure. I can sometimes hear spirits. I promise I didn't die, but if we don't get moving quickly, I can't guarantee that won't be the case when we get there."

"Fine, but this discussion isn't over. You're not telling me everything."

Putting her hand on top of his, she looked Nolan in the eye. "I promise, later we can chat about all of this. We do need to get going, though."

Standing and stretching out her arms, she looked at the golems and Nolan. "Grab onto me, everyone. This may be a bit unsettling. Please, try to be quiet when we arrive in case someone is near."

Closing her eyes and taking a deep breath, she reached out to feel everyone's energy, tapping into theirs to take them with her. On the exhale, she pictured the side alley in the capital that she'd scouted and pulled the group through with her.

Iolite and Merit let go of Adalyn, looking around to ensure that they were indeed alone. Carnelian turned and dry heaved while Lazuli patted his back. "I don't know why you're doing that. We don't even eat. What do you think is going to come out?"

"Bugger off." Another dry heave jerked his body as he propped himself up on the wall. "Don't you think I know that? Magic and I don't get along."

Lazuli snorted, trying to contain a laugh. "Says the man made of enchanted stone."

Carnelian brushed off the hand on his back and stayed bent over for a few moments longer before straightening.

Adalyn realized Nolan was still holding her hand, staring at her face. She gave him a reassuring smile, squeezed his hand, and then let go. "Everyone, remember that stealth and recon is the plan. We cannot let anyone know we're here."

The group followed Adalyn as she worked her way up the alley toward the main street. As they got closer to the alley's entryway, more people appeared, all heading in the same direction. Backtracking, she whispered to the golems, "You said you had a way to be less noticeable? I don't see you going unnoticed out there as you are."

The golems looked to Iolite. "We do. I do request that what you are about to see stays between us. No one is to know that we are able to do this."

Adalyn and Nolan both nodded their agreement, watching intently as the golems each pressed and turned different stones on their bodies, causing each part to disappear.

"You're invisible!" Adalyn whispered excitedly. "Can people still touch you?"

Merit's disembodied voice responded, "They can. We will follow you as closely as possible. If we get separated, let's agree to meet back up where we arrived."

"Agreed. Nolan, are you ready to blend in?"

Checking the daggers in his boots and up his sleeves, since Adalyn had pointed out earlier that his long sword would be impossible to hide, he looked at her with a twinkle in his eye. "Let's do this."

The pair walked back up the alley and joined the crowd. Reaching out with her ability, Adalyn sensed the golems following them. They had spread out, with several tracing up nearby back alleys and one weaving in and out of the crowd around them as if they were smoke. Adalyn made a mental note to get to know the golems better. They clearly had some skills that could come in handy in a tight situation.

As they followed the flow of the crowd, more and more people joined, all heading toward the city center. An uneasy feeling grew as they got closer. The crowd was almost silent, and no one looked each other in the eye.

Upon reaching the center, the crowd stopped and joined a large gathering around a makeshift gallows. Soldiers surrounded it, preventing anyone from getting too close. Adalyn and Nolan worked their way through the crowd until they found a spot where they could be out of the way and have a good view of what was happening, with a quick exit if needed.

There was movement as the crowd parted off to the side and allowed a pack of soldiers through. When the group got to the center, they parted to show several men in varying levels of armor accompanied by four individuals in shackles.

Adalyn tried to lift herself up to see the faces of those who had just entered, but couldn't make them out over the heads of the people in front of her. "I'm going to move forward."

Nolan grabbed her shoulder. "Are you sure? If something happens, we can't get out of here without you."

"I'm not leaving any of you behind. You can come with me if you want."

Working their way through the crowd, they moved to the edge near the gallows. A deep, booming voice echoed through the center. "Thank you all for coming."

Adalyn caught a quiet mumble from someone behind her, "Like we had a choice." Suddenly, she understood why the crowd felt so uneasy. This was a mandatory appearance. Whatever was about to happen, they wanted witnesses.

"Defiance is not tolerated," the voice continued without preamble. "These four have been found guilty of rebellious behavior and will be executed. We are not unkind, but we do expect obedience." The man stepped back while another man in armor stepped forward. He turned in Adalyn's direction, and she suddenly couldn't breathe. She knew that face. She had worked with him since coming to the palace.

The four people in shackles were each escorted onto the stand and placed next to a noose. "Eric Knoflstead, you have been found guilty of rebellious behavior in the form of thievery."

That voice, it had to be him. Really him. It was Chef Staryn, but how did he get into the ranks of the Chors army?

A youth, barely older than a child, sniffled, trying to be brave as he turned and moved forward while the noose was placed around his neck. Murmurs and sniffs could be heard coming from various parts of the crowd. Adalyn's mind raced as she watched the events unfold, not believing what she saw taking place. There hadn't been a hanging in the capital since immediately after the Great War.

"Trayvil Mercurus, you have been found guilty of rebellious behavior in the form of espionage."

A broody, middle-aged man turned and stood tall as they moved him into the noose.

"Merideth Freeheart, you have been found guilty of rebellious behavior in the form of misdirection."

An old woman stepped forward while several people in the crowd wailed and shouted angrily. She gave them a loving look, as if to tell them that everything would be all right, even as the noose was placed over her head.

"Isabella Kayhelm, you have been found guilty of rebellious behavior in the form of physical ambush."

Adalyn gasped, and Nolan grabbed her as she lunged forward at the sight of her best friend on the stand. "You can't do anything," he whispered harshly. "Remember to stay hidden."

Adalyn jerked herself away from him and used her ability to transport herself next to Isabella. She couldn't let Isabella die, especially not like this. A soldier knocked her over as she reached out to grab her best friend. Drawing her short sword from its hiding place down her back under her cloak, she got back up. Defending herself the best she could from the soldiers rushing toward her, Adalyn pushed toward Isabella. A soldier had grabbed her bound hands and was pulling her toward the stairs, away from the conflict.

"Stop her!" Staryn hollered as he ran toward her from the opposite side of the gallows.

Shoving a soldier off the stand while pulling another off-balance, Adalyn rushed forward. "Isabella! Fight back! I'm coming for you!"

Isabella fell as she was dragged off the stage and laid still. The soldier tried to lift her, and Adalyn dove down on top of him. He kicked her off, threw Isabella over his shoulder, and disappeared into the panicked crowd, heading for a group of soldiers that was trying to get to the gallows, but were hampered by the masses around them. Adalyn gave chase, frantically pushing her way through.

"Isabella! Come back!"

She whipped around as a hand grabbed her arm. "Adalyn, stop! We have to get out of here." Nolan stared her down and grabbed her other arm as she struggled in his grip. "She's gone. Stop it! We need to meet up with the others before we get caught."

She glanced in the direction the soldier had gone and turned back to Nolan. "Fine, let's go."

NINETEEN

Adalyn collapsed to the ground, sobbing, as soon as she transported the group back to the common room. The golems quietly headed toward the dwarven dwelling as Nolan paced back and forth with clenched fists.

"Do you have any idea what you just did? How could you do something so selfish?"

"Selfish? Selfish! How is trying to save my best friend selfish?"

"Do you really not understand what you just did? Not only did you put the golems in danger of being discovered, but the enemy also now knows you and I both survived and that you have a magical ability."

"How do they know you survived? You didn't jump up there to help me!" She wiped her nose on her sleeve and stood, then stalked toward him, becoming angrier with each step.

"No, but Staryn knows my face, and I saved you from doing something extremely stupid! The chances of him not having seen me are very slim. Did it ever occur to you what would happen if they saw us? That now they may start torturing civilians or possibly even Isabella because they think someone must know about us? Did you think about this at all?" Nolan spat out at her, his face almost purple with anger.

Adalyn stared him in the eye, both ashamed and fuming. "I think you should go."

"To be honest, I don't want to be here right now, either. But this isn't over. We have a lot to discuss, and I'm not going to let this go. But right now, I need to report what just happened to the queen." With that, he turned on his heel and stomped back toward the dwarven settlement.

A moment of silence passed while Adalyn stared where Nolan had been, breathing hard and clenching her fists as tears continued to stream down her face.

"I told you taking company was a bad idea."

"Not now, Glenda. I'm not in the mood." Adalyn shifted her vision so she could see the spirits in the common room. The number seemed to have increased since she last looked.

"I understand, but this would have never happened if you had gone in your spirit form."

Wiping tears from her eyes and taking a deep breath to settle her nerves, Adalyn glared at Glenda. "I got it. I messed up. Drop it, though. It's my mess to fix, and I don't need to be reminded. I already feel bad enough."

As she turned toward the hallway, Glenda hollered, "Where do you think you're going?"

"My room. I need some space."

"Don't take too long. Your king needs to be notified of what just happened. Nolan is definitely heading to his queen to report what you just witnessed."

Clenching her fists, Adalyn walked out of the room without responding.

Even after taking the time to cool down, Adalyn still felt stressed. Screwing up her courage, she set out to find King Coeus. Informing him of the scouting fiasco once she'd found him went over about as well as her last conversation with Nolan had. The thorough haranguing she received left her feeling like a piece of laundry going through the wringer—repeatedly.

Once she was finally dismissed from the king's presence, and needing a break from people who wanted something from her, she sought out Eridu. Gathering herself before opening the door to the archives, she told herself that a friendly face was exactly what she needed right now.

The door creaked as she gently closed it behind her.

"Hello? Who's there?"

"It's Adalyn."

"Just who I wanted to see!"

"Where are you?"

"Walk straight forward from the door for seven aisles, then turn left. You'll find me."

Counting each row as she passed, Adalyn reached the seventh and paused. "Your left or my left?"

"What do you mean, my left or your left? You don't even know what my left would be. Your left."

With a mumbled apology, Adalyn turned down the aisle and continued until she came across Eridu in a small alcove with a table piled high with crates.

"You will never believe what I just found!" Eridu exclaimed, her face beaming.

"I truly have absolutely no idea."

"Look at these." Eridu shoved a pile of papers into Adalyn's hands. "They're maps."

"That's… interesting."

Eridu lifted her brow. "Interesting? These could change the course of this war! I've sorted through every crate I could find of them, and these," she said as she gestured to the pile around her, "are all maps of the tunnels between here and your capital."

Understanding dawned on Adalyn. "You mean these could give us entry points that we could possibly use for an attack?"

Eridu bounced up and down on the balls of her feet. "Yep! I told you I found something really big. These are incredible! Can you help me gather them to bring to the kings?"

"Why don't you let me take care of that?"

"I really don't mind."

"I know you don't. I just have a way to check these out without taking away manpower from getting ready for the actual attack."

"Are you going to ask Nolan or Venlian for help? There are a lot of tunnels."

Avoiding Eridu's eyes, Adalyn grabbed an armful of maps. "Venlian's busy helping the council."

Eridu stepped into Adalyn's view, "And Nolan?"

Adalyn looked at her pile of maps. "We may not be on speaking terms right now."

"You're joking. With all of the lovey eyes he gives you

when you're not looking, there's no way he is giving you the cold shoulder."

"I may have upset him."

"What did you do?"

Putting the maps back on the table and gesturing with her hands, she explained, "I may have almost gotten myself killed and possibly blown the fact that some of us are hiding somewhere."

"Wait, back up. Start from the beginning."

Adalyn recapped what had happened in the city. Going over the story again didn't lessen her shame any, and by the end she felt like hiding in her room and never coming out again.

"Nolan's kind of right, you know."

Adalyn heaved a sigh. "I know. I wasn't thinking, and I screwed up."

Eridu put a hand on Adalyn's arm. "Talk to him."

"I don't know if I can. You didn't see him."

"No, but I know when a person likes someone as much as he seems to like you, they tend to be more willing to listen and forgive."

"If I see him, I will apologize."

"And if you don't see him?"

"Fine, I will seek him out," Adalyn conceded. "Happy?"

"Perfectly. Now, help me gather all of the maps. We still have to get them to the kings, but I have duplicate copies you can look over."

TWENTY

Once she was back in the Banneret common room, Adalyn started laying the maps out. Shifting her vision so she could see the spirits in the room with her, she found Glenda nearby. "How well do you know the tunnels down here?"

The entire room laughed. Adalyn had learned that she was often the object of their attentions, as they found her appearances in the room diverting.

Glenda floated over to investigate the maps. "We lived down here," Glenda answered. "We know the tunnels very well."

"I don't know why I never thought to ask you about this before. Would you be willing to help me see which of these tunnels are still usable? If I could find safe ways for us to get our soldiers into the castle and city without being noticed, that would be a huge help."

Glenda gave her a knowing look. "Thinking it may help ease the king's anger after you gave away that there are people in hiding nearby?"

Adalyn kept her hands busy sorting through maps. "Maybe."

"I think that's smart. More and more spirits are showing up every day, including a lot of Banneret who lived here before. I will organize everyone to help check the tunnels. Can you spread out the maps so I can determine who goes to see which ones? It will be much easier to report back on locations with the individual maps, but we can't physically touch them."

"That's a great idea. Let me…" Adalyn froze at the sound of the door opening.

"I hoped I would find you here." Nolan entered the room. "What do you have here?"

Adalyn pulled a few maps to her chest and avoided his gaze. "Nothing."

"Really? We're keeping secrets now?"

She turned her head away from him and toward the wall and mumbled, "I'm not sure how much I want to share with someone who's mad at me."

Taking a step in her direction, Nolan fidgeted with his hands. "That's why I came to find you. Can we talk?"

"In a minute. First, can you help me spread these out individually?"

Taking a stack, Nolan looked up suddenly at Adalyn. "These are maps!"

"That they are. You're a smart one." She shot a glance up at him and realized the retort may have been a mistake.

He shuffled through the first few in his pile. "These are maps of the tunnels. What we wouldn't have done to get a hold of these when we first escaped the castle! Where did you find them?"

She let out a sigh of relief at him skipping over her sarcasm. "Eridu did."

"Shouldn't we bring them to our leaders and start checking them out?"

"They already have them. These are duplicates." Moving to one side of the room and laying them out on the floor, she added, "I had an idea. It won't use their resources, and we will have faster answers."

He joined her and began laying out the maps he held. "What's your idea?"

"You know how I can travel from one place to another and separate my spirit from my body?"

"Yeah."

"Well, there's more to worldwalking—my ability. I don't actually disappear from one spot and reappear in another. I kind of manipulate our world's reality." She'd gone over this with Glenda, and hoped it would make sense as she explained it to Nolan.

She held a map up in front of him. "Imagine this map is for where we are now. We're here," she said, putting a finger on a spot. "If I've been to a place before, or can see it, I sort of fold our world and step through." She pointed to another place with her other hand, then folded the map so the two spots met. "I create a shortcut." She paused to gauge his reaction across the room.

Nolan was slack-jawed. "That's... amazing."

"That's not all." Unfolding that map, she picked up another and laid it on top. "Imagine these are two different worlds, or layers of reality in the same place. I can see what's here or transport into the one in the same location. It's what I do when I travel with my spirit. The thing is, I'm not alone when I go to the other worlds. I can interact with whoever resides in that realm."

"Can you combine the two and change locations and worlds at the same time?"

Adalyn glanced at Glenda near the fireplace. Seeing Glenda nod, she responded, "Apparently, I can."

"Can you take people with you to other worlds, like you did with transporting the elves here?"

Again, Adalyn glanced at Glenda, who nodded back. "I guess I can do that, too."

"Can you—"

Adalyn cut him off. "I'm still figuring out my abilities. I've learned a lot, but I'm still learning how to use them fully."

"Sorry, I don't mean to pry. This is just exciting."

"It really is."

"One more question, and then I promise I'm done. When you go to other worlds, can you take your body with you, or does your spirit always leave it behind?"

As Adalyn looked at Glenda again, he stopped putting maps on the ground. "Why do you keep looking over there before answering me?"

"Um…" she stalled. How would he react to their conversation not being private? "We're not alone in here."

"What do you mean, we're not alone?"

"The room is technically full of spirits. Actually, most of the tunnels down here are."

He dropped his maps in surprise. "Show me," he said after a moment.

"I can't do that!"

"Yes, you can. You just said you can take people to other worlds with you. I want to see."

Letting out a big sigh, she directed him to the couch, where they both sat down. "Give me your hand and try not to freak out."

Adalyn closed her eyes, and he mimicked the behavior. She pulled him with her as she let go of her body, and their spirits began floating just above their bodies. "Open your eyes, Nolan."

His face lit up. "This is incredible! There are so many of them."

She looked around and noticed at least thirty sets of eyes all looking at them. Glenda chuckled. "They can see and hear you, as well. Technically, we've always been able to see and hear you. It's nice to finally meet you in person, Nolan. I'm Glenda, the last person to have had Adalyn's ability."

"Nice to meet you, too. You're the one who helped us find the dwarves, right?" She nodded, and he looked around the room again. "I really don't know what to say. Is this the afterlife? Why are there so many spirits here?"

"That's a long story that we really don't have the time to get into. For now, let's focus on our task at hand. If you wouldn't mind, finish laying out the maps so we can start investigating the tunnels."

Adalyn pulled them back into their bodies again. "Are you all right?"

"Yeah, that's an experience that's going to take a while to get used to," he responded, his face pale.

"It took me a bit of time to process, as well. Do you

want to work on that half of the room, and I will work on this half? If you need to, feel free to sit here for a minute first."

He nodded, looking like he was going to be sick.

TWENTY-ONE

Once the maps were assigned out for the first round of checks, Adalyn picked one up and headed toward the door.

Nolan stepped in front of her. "Where do you think you're going?"

"I may as well check one out as well. I don't have anything else to do today."

"You're not going alone. I'm coming with you."

"You've got the time? I'm not sure how long this will take."

"We still need to talk, too, remember?"

Adalyn had been hoping he would forget, and they could move past what happened while scouting without having to discuss it.

"All right, follow me. Let's get going."

They went through a maze of twists and turns, entering tunnels that clearly were all built at different times by different people. Some by humans, others by dwarves, and a few even showed some elven construction.

"Do you know where we're going?" Nolan asked.

"I'm following the map."

"Are we lost?"

Slightly irritated, she responded, "Again, we have the map. We can get back. Do you regret coming along?"

"No, I'm just starting to get hungry. Are we alone?"

She looked around them. "We are. I should probably start with the apologies, though. I hadn't been thinking of the consequences of my actions when I tried saving Isabella. She's my best friend, and I don't feel guilty for wanting to prevent her from being killed. She is the closest thing to family that I have." Glancing in Nolan's direction, she saw his scowl. "I do regret having put all of you, as well as our chances of taking back the capital, in danger. I especially owe you an apology for how I behaved directly after. I was distraught and angry—at myself, for not having thought of the consequences, and at you, for pointing them out to me. It wasn't fair of me to lash out at you."

Nolan was quiet for a moment, allowing Adalyn time to continue in case she wasn't done. "I appreciate that. I should have handled how I approached you about it differently. Your actions weren't because you are a bad person. I know you weren't trying to cause problems. I do think the fact that we almost got killed had me a bit on edge, and I directed that fear toward you."

"I failed," Adalyn whispered.

Nolan stopped her, grabbing both of her arms. "Look at me."

She looked up, her eyes glistening.

"You did not fail," Nolan said. "No, Isabella wasn't

rescued. But last we saw, she was still alive. While some of the results were not what we wanted, you are clearly doing what you can to repair that. You are a good person," he said, releasing her arms. "Don't forget that."

She wiped away a tear and straightened. "Thank you." Offering her hand between them, she asked, "Forgiven?"

He grasped her hand and smiled. "Always."

They continued along the tunnels, investigating rooms along the way. She made notes of several holding weapons that might be useful after some repair, while Nolan pointed out rooms that were large enough to stage troops in before the attack began. Several rooms caught her interest simply because there were no cobwebs or dust. Adalyn wryly thought that she was in need of that kind of magic now. After hours of pulling the fine-spun threads out of her hair and choking on clouds of dust kicked up from their investigations, they were covered in grime from head to toe.

Turning a corner, the two encountered a collapsed section, blocking them from going any further into the tunnel. A glow from one of the doors near the end caught Adalyn's attention, and they moved closer.

"Wow," she whispered.

From the doorway, a cavern opened up with a small body of water in the center. Glowing blue and green rocks filled the room, their calming glow reflected on the water.

"This is incredible," Nolan said, taking a step into the room.

"It's pretty magical."

He chuckled. "Knowing all of the weird stuff that we've found, it probably is magical."

"Good point." Taking one last look, she turned leave. When Nolan didn't join her, she looked back at him. "What are you doing?"

Slipping off a boot and starting on the other, he gave her a devilish grin. "There's no way I'm not getting in this. You've dragged me all over these tunnels. I'm going to soak and relax before we head back."

"We don't even know if it's safe."

Stripping down to just his underclothes, he tested the water before stepping in. "It feels pretty great. Must be a hot spring nearby."

She turned her back on him and huffed. "Are you sure we have time for this? I thought you were hungry."

"I am hungry. This will only take a few minutes, though. Join me."

"I don't have anything to wear."

"You say that like it's an issue."

She blushed and glanced back at him. "That's easy for a guy who has the body of a god to say."

He wiggled his brows and with a wicked grin retorted, "Says someone with the body of a goddess. Keep on as much as you want, just get in here and join me. It feels incredible."

Trying not to look at his perfectly chiseled form, she moved to the side of the water and removed her outerwear. She dipped a toe in, and her body begin to relax immediately. Sinking the rest of her body in sent a tingle through her.

"Feels great, doesn't it?"

The tension from her shoulders and neck began to release as she allowed the water to run through her fingers while moving her arms back and forth. Taking a few steps further into the pool, her feet never slipped on the smooth, hard surface.

"It really does."

She stared through the crystalline water, shimmering and clear, watching the way the lights cast shadows through the water onto her flesh.

"You can look at me, you know. I'm not shy."

Her brain started to overthink his last comment. "I don't know if that actually makes me feel better."

A splash caught her by surprise, and she turned quickly on Nolan. "You didn't!"

The twinkle in his eye and giant grin told her that he got exactly the response he was looking for. He sent a large splash in her direction again.

"Oh, you're going to regret that!"

The two splashed each other for a few moments, with Nolan moving closer each time. Once within arm's reach, she bounced up and shoved him fully under the water. Grabbing onto her waist, he pulled her under with him. Both emerged holding onto each other, sputtering.

Nolan reached up and moved her hair out of her face. Her heart raced in her chest as he pulled her even closer, their lips almost touching. "I want to kiss you," he murmured. "If I should stop, please say something now."

Reaching with both hands, she cupped his face and looked into his eyes. Shaking her head, she leaned in and kissed him. Melting into each other's arms, their kiss deepened. His hand moved to the small of her back and pulled her close to his chest, while the other cupped her head.

Nolan yelped and suddenly pulled away. "Something is touching me!"

Startled, Adalyn looked down at the water and noticed small, glowing bugs swimming in the water around them. Laughing, she teased Nolan with a wink. "I thought you wanted to kiss me so badly. Letting a little bug scare you away?"

His scowl as he got out of the pool told her everything. "You know I don't like bugs."

Adalyn took her time getting out of the water, watching Nolan shake the droplets from his body. He began putting his clothes back on.

"You sure you want to do that while you're still wet? It's a long, cold walk back. You're going to get blisters."

"I'm not staying here. I can still feel them on me."

She finished climbing out and got dressed. She caught up to Nolan in the hallway, then stopped suddenly and pointed. "Looks like you have a little follower there."

Spinning in a circle, he swatted at every inch of his body. "Where? Get it off."

A grin spread from ear to ear as she shook her head, "This is never going to get old."

Shooting her a dirty look, he smirked. "Maybe not for you. Look, anyone is going to act squeamish if they're naked."

"I see your point. Ready to head back?"

Giving one last shiver, he straightened. "Let's go. We can mark this tunnel off and grab some food. Maybe talk about what just happened?"

She just nodded and followed him, not entirely sure

how she felt about what had happened in the glowing room with the pool.

Arriving in the common room, Glenda gave the two a once-over. "What have you two been up to?"

Adalyn plopped down on a chair and tried to wipe the blush off her face. "We found a pool of water in a glowing cave. The tunnel beyond it was collapsed, though."

"Ah, I know of that cave. It's beautiful, isn't it? I'm glad you can still access it. There are a lot of places like that hidden down here in the tunnels. We've got a few of them to show you that are still accessible." Glenda walked around the room, pointing at different maps as Adalyn wrote notes about what the Banneret had found. "I really think you should look at some of these yourself, so you can give a report as to the size and condition of the open tunnels to the king."

"Now?" Adalyn asked.

"You can wait if you need to, but I think this information would be best given to your king sooner rather than later," Glenda answered.

Adalyn explained what Glenda had said to Nolan as he sat on the couch and laid out the maps in piles by order of importance, since he couldn't see the spirit at the moment. "Do you want to grab some food first?" he asked. "It would give you a chance to rest and recharge."

"As fantastic as that sounds, I should go look at the tunnels now. I'm about to fall asleep just sitting here, and if I wait much longer before I get moving, I'm not going anywhere. Glenda, where to first?"

Adalyn left her body in the common room and followed Glenda in spirit form. After being shown two small tunnels that connected to old cellars and a larger tunnel that opened into the sewer system below the capital, Adalyn stopped Glenda as they began their final tunnel. "Are we near the cells?"

"You've got a good memory. We are. They connect into this system."

"Couldn't we use that one?"

"Do you remember how narrow those passages were? You wouldn't be able to get a large enough number of people in there to push your way outside. The cells themselves are not heavily guarded, but they whittle down to paths so narrow that only one person at a time can go down them. The other paths are more likely to be useful."

"I understand. Can I ask a favor, though?"

"Possibly."

"Since we are so close, do you mind if I check on the cells in the dungeon?"

"You want to see if Isabella is back in them?"

Adalyn nodded, not trusting her voice.

"Of course. Let's go check on your friend."

The two of them glided down the halls and through the dungeon until they came upon Isabella's cell. There she lay, whip marks on her back, blood-crusted scraps of cloth sticking to her wounds. There was no movement from her body other than shallow breathing.

Tears fell down Adalyn's face and disappeared as they rolled off her cheeks. "She's hurt."

Glenda placed a hand on her back. "She's still alive because of you."

"Look at her, though. I wish I could help her."

After a moment of silence, Glenda quietly responded,

"Maybe you can. Currently, you're using your world-walking ability to separate your spirit from your body. This is quite literally your life force. Not all worldwalkers have this ability, but some are able to share their life force in a healing way. I don't know that it would heal her wounds in a physical sense, but it may help reinvigorate her system so she can heal more easily on her own, help her fight off infections and that sort of thing."

"Could you do it?"

"No. I wasn't blessed with, or at least, never developed that part of my ability."

Adalyn watched her best friend shiver on the stone floor. "I have to try. I can't leave her like this."

Moving next to Isabella, Adalyn looked at herself and her friend lying next to her. A wave of sadness encouraged her to lay down and hold her friend. Reaching out to feel her spirit's aura as if she was preparing to teleport her, an idea popped into her head. She attached to the aura and attempted to jump with Isabella.

Glenda looked skyward. "You know that's not going to work. Even you in your spirit form can't jump in here. We have to walk in and walk out, like everyone else."

"I had to try."

"I understand. Focus on what you can do. See if you can help your friend heal."

Unsure how exactly to go about it, she pictured her spirit hugging Isabella's spirit and sending as much love and hope as she could between them. She began to feel a shift in her spirit as small amounts of her life force moved between them.

"It's working. She's breathing better already."

Adalyn pushed more toward her friend.

"Be careful. You don't want to give too much. This is your actual life force you are sharing. It will take time to regenerate, and if you go too far, there's no coming back. I won't be able to help you."

She held on for a moment longer.

"Adalyn, you need to let her go. She is doing much better now. Look at her."

Pulling herself away, she could see color back in Isabella's face. She reached up to stroke her face, content with the now peacefully sleeping figure in front of her.

"Thank you."

"Of course. We should go. I still need to show you the rest of the last tunnel, and you look about finished."

Forcing herself to float back over to Glenda, she turned back one last time. "Goodbye, Isabella. Next time, I'm coming back to get you out of here. Don't give up."

TWENTY-TWO

Adalyn had no idea where she was. She was somewhere in the mountains, but they didn't look like the mountains around the capital. These looked younger, taller, and had sharper peaks. Everything seemed unusually still, as well. No birds were chirping, even though it was the middle of the day. No sounds came at all, now that she thought about it. The sun was high and hot, making her shift uncomfortably in her nightdress.

Slowly walking toward a tight grouping of trees, the silence was broken by a crackling noise followed by a loud pop. Adalyn hurried to see where the noise had come from.

A golden orb glowed brightly from a grove deeper within the woods. Curious, she slowly walked toward the light, pausing after just a few steps when a figure appeared. A man stepped out of the orb's light, covered in a hooded, dark green robe. Three more figures followed him out of the light and into the grove. Each of them wore the same type of robe with the hood pulled up to hide their faces.

Not wanting to be seen, Adalyn crouched down to watch and wait. The group gathered in a circle and started to chant words she didn't understand. The first one to arrive pulled a book out of his cloak and opened it.

Holding something from among the pages up to the sky, a strangely familiar voice chanted louder than the rest. His deep pitch felt like home to her, but she didn't know why. The object he held caught fire, and the group grew silent and stepped back from each other. The fiery object floated back down to the book, resting on the open pages. A burst of energy shot from the book in every direction with such force it knocked her onto her back.

Her vision darkened and her ears rang. She rolled over to make sure the group hadn't noticed her when she fell. To her relief, they were all distracted. What were they doing?

Lying on the ground, she watched as they congratulated each other, chatted for a few minutes, and then said their farewells. Her eyes drooped, and she fought to keep them open. The first man turned and headed up a path toward the mountains, while the rest of the group walked back through the light and disappeared. Adalyn couldn't hold on any longer and gave in to the pull of unconsciousness.

WAKING UP IN HER BED CONFUSED ADALYN FOR A minute. Was it another dream, or possibly worldwalking? Her heart beat hard in her chest.

Spending so much time in the tunnels had worn her out entirely. By the time she was done, she had skipped eating and fallen asleep as soon as her head hit her pillow. She didn't know how to tell the difference yet between worldwalking in her sleep versus just dreaming, but after how vivid her dream had been, she was determined to find out.

Her stomach growled, demanding food before she did anything else. Deciding she wouldn't be able to fall back asleep anyway, she climbed out of bed and headed to the dining hall to grab some warm food before seeking out Glenda.

One of the biggest issues with living underground was the inability to tell time. The dwarves had clocks that their society functioned by, but living apart from everyone else also meant that some days Adalyn functioned on a very different schedule. She realized this had to be one of those moments when she walked in to find the dining hall empty and the fires banked.

Turning to leave, the sound of a chair scuffing on the floor startled her.

"I'm sorry. I didn't mean to scare you. You don't have to leave." Venlian gestured to a plate in front of him. "I found some bread and cheese that I'm willing to share, if you care to join me."

Moving to sit across from him, she picked up a piece of the bread. "Thank you." Noting his unusually disheveled hair, she asked, "What has you up so late tonight?"

"I'm going over some final preparations for taking the capital back. No one can decide on a plan of attack that has a very strong chance of success."

Choking on the dry bread, she grabbed a chunk of the cheese and tossed it in her mouth, which only made her mouth feel even drier, and her coughing worsened.

Venlian chuckled and slid his mug across the table. "Take a drink."

She eyed him and decided that ultimately dying was worse than drinking from the same cup as him. "Thank you again." She cleared her throat. "I actually have something that may help. Eridu found maps of the tunnels leading from the Banneret barracks to the city. Nolan and I have been checking them out. Several are still in good working order and could be used to get our people in."

His eyebrow rose. "You and Nolan checked them?"

"We had a little help from some spirit friends of mine, but yes. I was planning on bringing the maps to the king later today."

"Do you mind showing me? After you finish eating, of course."

"They're in the common room. We can go get them…" She stood and shoved another bite of bread in her mouth, then gagged when she tried to swallow too soon.

"Maybe slow down for a second. We're in no rush."

Sitting down again and taking another drink, a thought popped into her head. "You told me I had visited you before in my dreams, right?"

"I did."

"What was that like?"

"What do you mean?"

"Was I in a spirit form or a physical body?

"You always came as a spirit, but not like a ghost. You always appeared in a way where I could see you, but you tried to interact with all objects like you were there in your physical body."

"Hmm… interesting. I wonder if because I didn't realize what I was doing, maybe I kept the restraints of my physical body, even when I worldwalked in my dreams."

"That's a strong possibility. From what I know of your ability, you have much more control over how you appear than you know. You have a very powerful ability, and I think you're creative enough to figure out unique ways to use it."

"Venlian, is that a compliment?" Adalyn teased.

"More of an encouraging moment."

"All right, I will take what I can get. Thank you for this."

"The food?"

"The conversation as well."

"Anytime. If you're finished, we can head up so you can show me what you've found."

Downing the last of the bread and brushing the crumbs off her lap, she gave him a big grin. "Absolutely! Let's get going."

TWENTY-THREE

Things moved quickly after that. Between the troops King Coeus and Queen Tillie had gathered outside the capital during the weeks the expedition was gone, the awakening of the golems, and the aid of the elves, they had amassed quite a military force. The weapons that had been found in the old dwarven city and tunnels, not to mention what the elves brought with them, was sufficient to arm the troops with confidence.

The Banneret's discovery of a number of tunnels that led to strategic locations was happily received, and scouts were sent to each to evaluate them. Each report came back enthusiastic and optimistic, and the strategists went to work on finalizing plans.

The appointed day arrived, and Adalyn found herself looking at the capital from just inside the tree line as they waited for the signal to attack. The three towering walls and gates breaking up each stage of the city and crawling up the mountain mocked her. If she failed, the entire attack would fail. The dwarves, golems, and King Coeus were attacking from the tunnels and hidden entrances to the castle and upper city. Nolan was part of the private guard for Queen Tillie, who was leading the human troops alongside the elves from the lower gates. None of that mattered, though, if Adalyn couldn't transport her team into the gatehouses to allow their army in. The forces in the tunnels should be able to take the castle, but without the support from the troops outside the walls, they'd find themselves under siege.

"Are you anxious?" Venlian asked as he approached Adalyn's side.

"A little." Maybe if she downplayed her nerves, they would lessen in truth.

"Remember, you're not alone. Your ability has gained strength and become more reliable as you transported the elves here. You've prepared for this specifically by scouting where you are needed in spirit. You can do this."

Adalyn eyed the first gate. "I don't know. What if I have to kill someone? I've trained with the sword, but I've never taken a life. I trust my ability, but I've never had to use it in battle. There is just so much that could go wrong if I screw up."

"You can do this. I have faith in you, as do the rulers of these kingdoms."

"You wouldn't lie to me, would you? Just to make me feel better?"

"Elves can't lie."

"Says an elf," Adalyn said with a wink, trying to lighten the mood. She noticed Venlian's face reddening as he turned away from her.

A bird call followed by several others signaled the start of the attack. Soldiers poured from the trees toward the city, and three elven hands touched Adalyn as she drew her sword and pulled them with her into the gatehouse of the first wall. Three guards in the room stood in response to their sudden arrival, immediately clashing with Venlian and the two elven guards.

Adalyn rushed to the levers and opened the gate, the clanking of chains and gears drowning out the other sounds in the room.

Venlian drew his sword out of a guard's chest and signaled for them to follow him outside. The sound of clashing swords and people finding shelter from the chaos stunned Adalyn for a moment. A child's cry nearby snapped her out of her daze. Searching for the source of the sound, she found a toddler in the road surrounded by steel-wielding men unaware of the child's presence.

Ducking, dodging, and shoving soldiers out of the way, she reached the child only to be knocked down on top of it by the fighting. She clutched the child to her chest and stood. Bodies and weapons jostled them as she tried to get her bearings.

A Chors soldier rushed at her with a scream of anger. She held the child close in one arm and worldwalked to just behind the attacker, and then slashed her sword through his calf. She turned and ran as he fell to the ground.

Keeping low, she dodged through the crowd toward a set of houses. Opening the first door she came to, she considered leaving the child there alone, but decided that it was too close to the battle. Working her way away further from the fighting she caught the glimpse of a skirt disappearing around a corner. Hurrying after, she heard the sound of a door closing ahead. Slowing to a cautious walk and shifting the crying child to her hip, she found a building with citizens sheltering inside and opened the door.

"Does anyone know this child?"

"I do!" A plump woman with an apron came forward. "I will help her find her mother."

Handing the child to the woman, Adalyn shut the door behind her and headed back to the battle.

She paused just shy of the fight to look for Venlian. In the center of the battle, his silver and white armor glinted in the sun. His swords gracefully struck their intended targets as if he was dancing. She worldwalked near him, careful to avoid the blades as they regrouped for the next stage. She fought her way forward with him, the two of them sticking close as their army worked its way up the mountain.

As the group neared the second wall, Adalyn hollered at Venlian, "Where are the other two?"

He struck a soldier in the hamstring. "They fell behind."

"We can't wait for them."

Venlian nodded, kicked a soldier away from him, and pushed himself into Adalyn's back. As soon as they touched, she pulled them to the second gatehouse and immediately attacked the three guards on duty.

Venlian rotated to pull two of the soldiers to one side while Adalyn crossed swords with the third. Taking a hit to her thigh, she stumbled against the table and threw her sword up to defend another oncoming attack. The hit deflected. She retaliated with everything she had, plunging the sword into his mass. Her sword sank deep into his gut. The man collapsed to the ground, struggling to breathe until he stilled. Nausea hit Adalyn, and she gagged as she realized what she'd just done.

She leaned back on the table as Venlian finished off the other two and opened the gate. He headed toward the door, stopping when he realized she wasn't following him. Spotting the blood running down her leg, he moved next to her.

"Can you stand?"

"I don't think so."

He checked the wound, then looked up at her gravely. "I'm going to try something. Stay absolutely still."

As he touched her wound, a wave rolled through her, making her nausea worse. Turning suddenly to avoid Venlian, she threw up the small amount of breakfast she had forced herself to eat.

"You all right?"

Closing her eyes, she shook her head. "Not in the slightest."

Noting the dead soldier next to him, he touched her leg again and sent a softer wave that made her body relax. "How about now?"

"I do actually feel a bit better."

"Move your leg."

It still hurt, and she couldn't stand on it, but the bleeding had stopped and didn't begin again as she moved it.

"It's only a temporary fix, but at least you won't bleed

out." He went to the fireplace and grabbed a poker, bringing it back to her. "Use this to hold yourself up."

"You're joking."

"Do you have any better suggestions?"

"I can't walk. What good will this do?" she spat out, waving the poker at Venlian.

"It's only to keep you upright. You don't need to walk."

His meaning suddenly hit her, and she decided to give it a try. Leaning heavily on the poker, she used her ability to jump from the table to the fireplace. "I can do this, but I don't know for how long."

"Let's get moving. Stick to the sides of the battle. I will keep up with you, so don't wait for me. Head directly to the next gate."

She transported herself to the door, peeked out, and then transported to an open spot along the edge of the battle next to a building to hide. Adalyn jumped from shadow to shadow with the flow of the charging army so as to not get ahead of them. If she entered the gatehouse, she would be overrun without the soldiers flowing through the two open gates. This was the last one she needed to open before their armies from above and below would meet, if everything went according to plan. Knowing her luck, that wasn't likely to happen.

Hiding in an alley, she watched as the elves pushed through the enemy, getting closer to the gate. Venlian slid in next to her, touched her shoulder, and nodded, and she transported them inside the gatehouse. After defeating the soldiers and opening the gate, she peeked out the door to see what was happening.

A glimpse of a face she knew froze her in place.

"What's wrong?" Venlian asked, walking over to join her while adjusting his armor.

"Is it…?" she murmured to herself. The face flashed in the crowd again, moving toward a government building in the square. "It's him!"

"Who?"

"Staryn, he's out there! We can't let him get away." Pointing to where her former chef was heading, she touched Venlian's arm and pulled him with her to block his path. Losing her balance for a moment as Venlian pulled away to engage, she saw Queen Tillie and her guards surrounded by Chors soldiers and death slaughs.

Staryn evaded Venlian and dashed for the door. Venlian chased him into the building as Adalyn tried to decide what to do. Should she follow and help Venlian, or assist Queen Tillie? Glancing back at the queen, a gap opened as Nolan was hit in the head and went down. That made her decision for her.

Adalyn transported herself into the center of Queen Tillie's group, pulled them all toward her, reached her foot out to touch Nolan, and then pulled them all into the doorway of the building that Staryn had escaped into.

"You three, block and guard this door! Don't let anyone in!" Queen Tillie commanded. Turning toward Adalyn, she nodded in thanks. "We need to secure the rest of this building while our soldiers catch up. It's not safe to go back out there until more of our men are up here."

Adalyn glanced down at Nolan, who was being tended by another guard, and quickly looked away, swallowing.

"Venlian chased Staryn into this building. We need to find them."

Queen Tillie commanded her remaining guards, who headed into the building to clear it. Adalyn transported her way through the building, looking for Venlian. Entering an office, she found Staryn looming over Venlian's unconscious body.

"No!" Adalyn lunged, her anger taking over, and knocked Staryn down, pummeling him with her fists.

He rolled her off of him and lunged at her with his sword. Using her ability, she jumped from spot to spot, dodging his attacks. Knowing that she didn't have a chance if she fought fairly, she jumped above Staryn. He tried to dodge, but he wasn't quick enough.

They tumbled to the ground, and Adalyn turned and thrust with her sword. It was pure luck that she actually struck true, and Staryn shrieked as the blade pierced his side.

Adalyn worldwalked to the desk, using it as a barrier between them. She leaned on it and breathed heavily, taking the weight off her leg as she watched Staryn. He tried to get up but failed, moaning and clutching his wound.

Unsure what to do, Adalyn stayed where she was, watching as Staryn's face screwed up in pain. His eyes were closed against it, but then they opened and searched her out.

"Adalyn," he groaned, "I've known you since you first came to the castle. I took you in when your family disappeared and the money ran out." He yelled as another wave of pain wracked his body. "Helping Chors was all I could do to stay alive after they attacked. I didn't want to, but I had to," he said when the wave had passed, a few tears glistening on his cheeks. "I was just waiting for my chance to escape."

"Is that why you were trying to hang Isabella? You know her!"

"I was commanded to. I knew it was either her or me."

She shook her head, not sure what to believe, and transported over to check on Venlian. Good, he was still alive. Her gaze shot toward Chef, who still pleaded with his eyes.

"Lies," Adalyn spat. His pitiful appearance now didn't change what he'd done.

"No, I swear it!"

"Oh, you swear?" Safe for the moment, her emotions let loose, and anger rose to a raging inferno inside her. "You swear, do you, Nightshade?"

All remaining color in Staryn's face drained away. The change had hardly occurred, however, when a wicked smile replaced the pouty tears. "You know about that, do you?"

Twisting her sword into the ground as she stood from her crouched position by Venlian, Adalyn looked down at him. "I was there when you broke the spell on the gateway. I didn't figure it out then, but I've since begun to piece the parts of the puzzle together. You had that day off, and no one knew where you went. You came out of the attack on the castle unscathed, with a rank in the Chors military, as well. No army is going to let an enemy suddenly join their ranks and give them a promotion. I even have my suspicions about how Jeb really died. I just don't get why."

"Ah, Jeb," Staryn sighed. "He was just in the wrong place at the wrong time. All this has been a long time coming." He coughed and spit out blood, shifting to sit. "When that spell was cast, ending the war, they didn't care about who was left where. They abandoned their soldiers in Chors and hunted down everyone left in Pieriun."

"What does that have to do with you?"

A smirk spread across his face. "The king didn't do a thorough job. A number of the Chors soldiers went into hiding and started trying to figure out how to break the spell. The job passed down from generation to generation."

"You were the smart one who figured it out, huh?"

He grinned. "I did."

"You know it's not completely fixed, right?"

His smile faltered for a moment. "That's not true. The Chors soldiers being here proves that."

"True, but the spell isn't entirely broken. There's a time difference. If you requested backup right now, it would take months before they got here to help."

"That can't be right. I did all the calculations. You're lying!"

"Am I? Have you had any reinforcements since the capital was taken over?"

"No, but we didn't request any."

"Is that so?"

He glowered at her, his silence speaking volumes.

Hearing footsteps in the hallway and Queen Tillie's commanding voice, Adalyn called, "In here!"

The queen and her guards entered the room. "What should we do with him?" one guard asked as another bound Staryn's hands. "We need to finish clearing the building. Both sides of our army are beginning to converge on the square."

Queen Tillie surprised Adalyn by looking to her. "What would you have us do?" she asked, her gaze assessing.

"Can you help me move him? He is a traitor, and I want him in the dungeon, but can't transport him the whole way," Adalyn asked.

Queen Tillie nodded and gestured two of her guards forward. Staryn struggled as they pulled him to his feet and was rewarded with a hit over the head with the pommel of one guard's sword.

Adalyn looked back at Queen Tillie. "We will be right back. Please, take care of Venlian." The guards carried Staryn over to her, and they transported to the entrance of the dungeons.

A single soldier at attention next to the gate attacked them as soon as they appeared. The rest must have joined the fight above. One of the queen's guards jumped into action and disarmed the Chors soldier, then took his keys and opened the door. Both guards looked to Adalyn expectantly.

"Unlock the cells, and throw both of these into one," Adalyn ordered. "Tell the people that although they are free, they need to stay here for now. There is still fighting above, and they would be in danger up there until it's over. We'll let them leave as soon as it's safe."

The guard nodded at her and started opening cells.

Excited and worn-out cries of joy echoed in the stone corridors as the prisoners realized what was happening. Adalyn slid down the wall at the dungeon entrance and rested as her orders were carried out, unable to move much due to her wounded leg, and too exhausted to, anyway.

As the crowd gathered and mingled in the dungeon, someone pushed through to the door.

"Adalyn?"

She looked up, surprised someone was addressing her by name.

"It's really you! You look absolutely terrible."

Adalyn groaned as Isabella bumped her leg, then knelt next to her. "You don't look much better, you know."

"Being stuck in a cell for the last few months will do that to a girl."

Both girls laughed weakly and hugged each other.

"I need to head back," Adalyn said regretfully, "but I promise we'll talk as soon as this is all over." Isabella nodded, though Adalyn could see the questions in her eyes.

Groaning, Adalyn shifted to stand. One of Queen Tillie's guards appeared next to her. "Need help?"

Holding her hand out for him, he hoisted her to her feet, and she transported back.

TWENTY-FOUR

"I see they're keeping you here to make sure you stay off that leg for a while," Eridu said as she entered the castle infirmary. "You know, we have stuff that could help it heal faster."

Adjusting the blankets on the bed and scooting over to make room for her friend to sit, Adalyn smiled. "You're so sweet. I'm fine, really. There are others who need it more than I do."

Eridu gave her a knowing smile. "If you change your mind, just ask."

Toying with the blanket in her fingers, Adalyn quietly inquired, "Have you heard anything about Nolan or Venlian? Last I saw, they were both unconscious."

"Nolan has already been released. I'm surprised he hasn't been in to see you yet."

"I'm sure, with everything going on, he has just been busy. What about Venlian?"

"The elves have their own infirmary set up in the forest. He is there."

"Is he all right?"

"They've been pretty tight with security there, so I haven't been able to get in to see him. Maybe once you get fixed up, they will let you into their camp. You seem to have formed some sort of a bond with them."

"Maybe," Adalyn said, reflecting on the interactions she'd had while transporting the elves to Pieriun. "I will definitely try."

"I should return to my duties, but if you need anything, don't hesitate to send for me."

"I will. Thank you, Eridu."

With a twinkle in her eye, Eridu shrugged. "What are friends for?"

Sitting in the infirmary for the next day was pure torture as Adalyn wondered what was happening in the aftermath of the battle. When she was finally released and summoned to see King Coeus, she practically bounced off the bed—until she put pressure on her leg. Then she collapsed and second-guessed if she should really be getting up at all. After picking herself up off of the floor with a chagrined smile for the infirmary attendant, she found a walking stick and made her way to see why she was needed. The butterflies in her stomach were going crazy as she wondered if the summons was a good or a bad thing.

She didn't think the occupants of the castle would take very well to her using her ability to suddenly appear places, so she set off on foot. Wiping the sweat from her brow outside the throne room, she questioned that decision, as well. Straightening herself the best she could, she nodded at the guard, who opened the door and announced her arrival. A small crowd filled the room, most of them with bandages of some sort, proving their participation in the battle.

"Come forward, Adalyn Mernt," King Coeus directed from his throne.

Hobbling up to stand in front of him with her head held high, she never lost his gaze. She couldn't read what was happening from his face. A tickling sensation encouraged her to shift her vision partially to see that the room was not only full of people in her own realm, but was also filled with spirits, all watching her. Something big was happening, she just didn't know what.

Reaching the throne, she stopped and attempted to bow. "I'm sorry, Your Majesty. My leg makes it difficult to bow."

"Not to worry." He raised his chin, a broad smile on his face. "Adalyn Mernt, you have proven to be loyal and valuable to the Pieriun kingdom and to me. I wish to acknowledge your deeds and the part they played in regaining the capital."

"Thank you. It's something I think most of your loyal subjects would have done if given the chance."

"Perhaps, but none had the skills necessary or took the opportunity to do what you did. Do you remember our discussion of the Banneret?"

Unsure if she liked where this was going, she hesitantly replied, "I do."

"You have been gifted with the ability of a Banneret and have used it in defense of the crown. I would like to reinstate the order of the Banneret and have you head up the re-creation of the unit as its captain. With the living spell in decline and magic being more openly accepted, I'm sure others will soon manifest abilities as you have, and I will need someone to help train and organize them. Do you accept this position?"

Stunned, she stared at him for a moment. "I'm not qualified to lead the Banneret," she blurted out.

"Do you see anyone else here with magical abilities?"

"Well, no. That doesn't mean I should be leading them, though."

The frown on the king's face clearly told her that he normally didn't have people refuse him and wasn't pleased. "If you turn this down, I will be forced to place either a non-magical person in charge, or a magical person I do not know. While you may have no experience as a leader, you are still my best choice. Do you understand?"

"I understand," she said meekly.

"So, do you accept?"

Not seeing any way to get out of it, she nodded in agreement.

King Coeus' face lit up, an entirely different expression from the frown he'd worn a moment before. "Good! As the new captain, I have your first mission decided. Take a few days to recover and begin organizing and preparing for new recruits, but then I need you to gather a party and go to Chors as an envoy. You will go to their king and persuade them that the war is long over and there is no need to attack."

Eyes wide, Adalyn grasped at the first thing that came to mind. "What, uh, what about the time difference?" she stammered.

"Ensure that you have someone you trust here to help

take care of new recruits as they arrive. While it will be difficult on our end, it will work in our favor for potentially getting this resolved before another serious attack occurs."

"I can choose my own party and who stays here to fill my place while I'm gone?"

"You're the captain now. These are your decisions to make."

Adalyn nodded, still a bit awestruck. "Thank you. I'm honored."

"You've done well. I look forward to seeing what you do with this new responsibility." With a nod of his head, he signaled that their conversation was over.

As Adalyn left the room, she noted the mix of facial expressions from the living and the overjoyed reactions of the spirits. Seeing Glenda step into her line of sight and motion for her, she followed her into a side room further down the hall, where the two of them were alone.

"Congratulations!" Glenda said with a big grin as Adalyn closed the door behind her.

Lowering herself slowly into a chair, Adalyn replied, "Thanks. To be honest, I'm not entirely sure what I just got myself into."

"No need to worry. You've got me. You've actually got a bunch of the Banneret spirits here who can help. It will be a bit unorthodox, but we can make it work. You can help bring people to our realm, and we can match up abilities and help them. Over time, some of the Banneret will return from Chors, and…"

"Wait. What?"

"You didn't think that there would be Banneret still in Chors?"

Adalyn paused a moment to consider this. The living spell had essentially frozen Chors in time, and King Dragmire had it enacted with no thought to where each armies' people were. Some of the Banneret must have been with the Pieriun army in Chors, so she supposed it made sense.

"This job just got much more intimidating," Adalyn said, her heart starting to patter even as she sat still. "I'm going to outrank people who have been a Banneret for much longer than me. I don't even fully understand my ability yet, and I will be expected to lead them."

"You'll be fine," Glenda assured her. "Plus, as long as we haven't figured out how to finish breaking the living spell, I will be around to help however I can."

"I'm sorry. I feel so bad that I haven't figured that out yet."

"Don't be. When the moment is right, it will be broken. For the time being, we will use the situation as it is to our advantage. Now, let's get you somewhere more comfortable and start figuring out who will take care of things for the Banneret here while you're gone."

GATHERED OUTSIDE THE GATEWAY IN THE DWARVEN tunnels, Adalyn triple-checked her bag. If she had learned anything from the last time she walked through this portal, it was that she wasn't prepared enough for everything that followed. Technically, she could just teleport with everyone, but she hadn't figured out how to jump just her spirit to Chors and scout the location first. No, using the gate was the best way to get there safely.

She felt a gentle touch on her back from Nolan. "You ready?"

"I think so." Standing, she threw the bag onto her back and walked over to Eridu. "I don't know how it's going to work with the new abilities showing up here, but if I come across Banneret or any of our soldiers in Chors, I will be bringing them back here. You're sure you don't need anything from me before I go?"

Adalyn had asked Eridu to be her second-in-command. While she was unlikely to ever have abilities appear herself, since dwarves couldn't wield magic, her experience in the archives would be beneficial in keeping records and finding useful information. She also knew more about how to manipulate magic than any human she could have chosen. Their kings had easily agreed to the idea and were thrilled at the idea of a dwarf being part of the Banneret. Eridu was a sort of ambassador in a way that no dwarf had been for over five hundred years.

"I will handle everything," Eridu replied. "No need to worry. Your mission is far too important to be worrying about things back here."

Adalyn embraced her friend. "There's no one I would trust more. Thank you."

They had decided to keep their return party small in hopes of traveling unnoticed to the king of Chors. Only Adalyn, Nolan, Venlian, and Vaeren would be on the mission. Traveling with the party from the original expedition made sense to Adalyn. She trusted them, and they each had experience that would be useful. Vaeren had been surprisingly beneficial in planning strategies for their battle to retake the capital, and Adalyn could see why the king valued him. He might not be the bravest person, but his mind was sharp. Nolan's scouting would help them as they moved through Chors, and Venlian had diplomatic experience that would aid them in the king's court.

Shifting the weight of her backpack, Adalyn moved to stand before Vaeren, Nolan, and Venlian. She glanced at them and reached out to the gateway with her ability, opening the portal. Glancing back one last time at Eridu, she gave a reassuring smile and stepped through.

The portal closed behind them as a blade appeared at Adalyn's throat.

"None of you move."

So much for traveling through Chors unnoticed.

The End

EPILOGUE

JOURNAL OF VENLIAN, KEEPER OF THE TOMES

I*2th Moon of the 46th cycle of the Red Crest*

My people are divided. Some are at a loss at what to do with this war. Others don't care and insist that we stay out of it. Let all humans wipe themselves out, they say. Still others are choosing sides in an effort to have it end sooner. Most of those choosing to join the fight are younger, of my generation.

I'm considering leaving our ancestral home to help stop the fighting and returning after. I love my libraries, but I feel as though I need to see a bit of the world, and I could contribute with the knowledge I have gained from reading the histories of so many campaigns in the past. Maybe I can be a warning to them.

The only thing is to decide whom to assist.

4TH MOON OF THE 47TH CYCLE OF THE RED CREST

I've chosen to help the kingdom of Pieriun. This war is

because the king of Pieriun's daughter married a prince of Chors and was to become queen. Soon after their wedding, she discovered that he had a pregnant mistress and was planning to name that child as his heir over any that the princess may have. According to the laws of both lands, she has every right to be upset and break the marriage contract. The prince of Chors disagreed and took it as a personal offense. How do you stop a war that was started over a broken heart?

I leave today for Pieriun's capital and will see if the king will accept my help, or if I am to be sent home to watch this play out.

5TH MOON OF THE 47TH CYCLE OF THE RED CREST

King Dragmire was very happy to see me arrive. Because of my experience, he didn't want to use me as a magical soldier, such as most elves who have chosen sides have become. Instead, I will be a member of his war council. I intend to use every bit of wisdom I've gained to help end this war quickly.

I am curious what they have already planned. This war has seen many battles in both kingdoms, and there has been little to no change.

23RD MOON OF THE 48TH CYCLE OF THE RED CREST

This has to be the least imaginative group of individuals on a war council that I have ever seen. I highly doubt that many, if any, have seen any sort of real battle before. Their own troops are seen as disposable pawns. Because of poor planning and insufficient training, I fear they may be too far gone for me to help them.

Dragmire's ventured too far into Chors and is losing men quickly. Some are just abandoning their posts once they get too deep and are cut off from retreating. Non-magical individuals are being thrown out as shields for those more powerful. Farm and country towns are being conscripted to fill the army. We need to teach these new recruits how to properly defend themselves and provide them with the correct type of armor and weapons to be able to fight those with magic. The king has no desire to spend from his coffers to cover that expense, however.

36TH MOON OF THE 48TH CYCLE OF THE RED CREST

The princess has joined the war council. It's important for her to learn how things work, but she is bringing her rage at the situation into the room and demanding attacks that our troops have no hope of winning. I haven't brought it up to the rest of the council, but I've had many of the elves I know inform me that they will be returning home. They are giving up on this war. Elves learned long ago how to step back when we were on the losing side. If only there was a way to show the king how to do that. At this point, I don't think the princess would let him.

Her rage for the dishonor she suffered from the prince consumes her thoughts. She mumbles about the mistress coming out of nowhere and enchanting the prince, stealing him away from her and turning the entire royal family against her. I begin to wonder if they are not the only ones potentially enchanted. Is this magic, or merely the rantings of a scorned and brokenhearted woman?

3RD MOON OF THE 49TH CYCLE OF THE RED CREST

The princess is starting to see how severe our losses have been. I think even the king is opening his eyes. I have reminded them that it's due to lack of training and proper supplies, as well as impractical planning for possible attacks, but all they see is that their people are being wiped out by magic. It's almost as if they forget that they have their own magical soldiers as well. If they used them well, they could still turn the tide of the war. I am afraid that my words are falling on deaf ears.

THANK YOU!

If you enjoyed this book, help an author out and leave a review and check out Book 2 —Dragonborn—soon to be released on September 20, 2022.

Bella's Marpleberry Muffins

Ingredients

1½ cups all-purpose flour
½ cup sugar
2 teaspoons baking powder
½ teaspoon salt
1 large egg
½ cup milk
1/4 teaspoon vanilla
¼ cup butter melted
1 cup marpleberries (blueberries if
marpleberries are out of season
1/3 cup butter softened
1/2 cup brown sugar
1/2 cup oatmeal
pinch of nutmeg

Stir together first 4 ingredients in a large bowl; make a well in center of mixture.
Stir together egg, milk, and melted butter until blended. Add to dry ingredients, stirring just until moistened. Fold 1 cup fresh or frozen blueberries, unthawed, into batter. Spoon batter into lightly greased muffin pans, filling two-thirds full. Combine softened butter, brown sugar, oatmeal and nutmeg until combined and slightly cubmly. Sprinkle on top of muffings and press gently ontop of the batter. You can press some of the crumble into the muffin with a knife as well.
Bake at 400° for 18 to 20 minutes. Remove from pans immediately.

Makes 12 muffins

ACKNOWLEDGMENTS

Thank you to everyone who has been part of this journey with me. The five years that it took to write this story has been such a learning curve and it wouldn't have happened without you.

My husband who I bounced ideas off of even though I wouldn't let him read it. Your insight and patience as I wrote late at night instead of crawling into bed to cuddle mean the world to me. There's a chance I just may let you read this eventually. If you see this, then congratulations!

My sweet baby girl. While this story is older than you are, it was your birth two, almost three years ago that really pushed me to start working on making this something that could go out into the world. This is my inheritance to you and something that I hope your children can enjoy in the future as well.

Mom, what would I do without you? My first reader and fan. I will always appreciate your thoughtful feedback and bouncing ideas back and forth as this random idea from a pinterest writing prompt became two stories which later were scrapped and combined to create this unique and fun world. Even if your daughter is a good writer, but has terrible grammar.

Dad, you I hope you know how much I appreciate everything you've done to try and help me make this dream come true. Your support means more than you could possibly know.

Kendra, without you this book would never have made it past the first draft. I was beyond overwhelmed at the amount of work ahead of me and if you hadn't given my hot mess of a draft a clean up I truly don't know if my brain would have ever allowed me to complete this book. I apologize again for handing you a draft that had every tense possible to write in.

Logan, your feedback and support gave me the courage to actually let this book baby of mine out into the world. The fact that you were willing to help teach me how to do that and get it into as many hands as possible means more than you can possibly know.

Jenny, you were my final key that I truly needed to make this happen. When I knew I needed to move onto the rest of Adalyn's story I wasn't quite sure how to fix this first one so I could show the world what her story really was. You are literally a miracle worker. You kept my story mine and polished it up in a way that I never dreamed was possible.

Clara, the beauty that you create when putting a book together is nothing short of a miracle. I love our nights sprinting together and all of the help that you've given me getting this story out to ARC readers means more than you know.

Angel, you were there when this story took off. I had been stalled almost half way through this book and letting me into your writing world and beginning to sprint with me is really what got me to the finish line.

My beta and ARC readers, you are amazing. So many

things about this story wouldn't be what it is if it wasn't for you. I appreciate the time, energy and forgiveness that you have had as this book slowly became the polished up version of itself. I can't wait to get to share what happens next with all of you!

ABOUT THE AUTHOR

Jamie Dalton is an author of YA fantasy. Growing up in Oregon and Idaho she fell in love with the magic of the mystery of the forests and history. After moving to North Carolina with her husband, her sass took on a life of its own and sassy magical fantasy stories began to be written. She fell in love with the publishing world and became a book cover designer as well as an author which she does during the night while her toddler sleeps. After all, it's called the witching hour for a reason.

If you do like her, (and I really hope you do!) you can follow her anywhere and everywhere.

Author website: Home | Author Jamie Dalton
Facebook author page: Log In or Sign Up to View
TikTok: Magnetra (@magnetra) TikTok | Watch
Magnetra's Newest TikTok Videos
Amazon profile: Jamie Dalton
Newsletter: Sign up
GoodReads: Reviews and purchase
Universal Purchase link for non US readers

www.ingramcontent.com/pod-product-compliance
Lightning Source LLC
Chambersburg PA
CBHW060307310726
48976CB00007B/2241